Mossy Creek
A Maggie Mercer Mystery Book 1
By Jill Behe

DevilDog Press

Edited by Rob Miller

Cover art by Dane@ebooklaunch

ACKNOWLEDGEMENTS

Thank you:

Monday Night Specials, without whom *Mossy Creek* wouldn't exist.

Rob M. Miller, editor and friend, for believing my words were worth the effort.

Tracy Tufo, for taking on this project through Devil Dog Press, and allowing my dreams to continue to flourish.

—Jill

Dedicated to:

Magdalena Elizabeth Susannah Maria-Louise Mercer … for a lot of things, but mostly for having a voice loud enough to rise above the din.

CHAPTER ONE
MONDAY MORNING....

"MORNIN', MAGGIE. SEEN the boss?"

I glanced up from my suspense novel, so engrossed, I hadn't heard the twenty-five-year-old rookie come in; a couple blinks brought me back to reality.

"Mornin', Officer Anderson. He's not in yet."

Because we're all on a first name basis, I *try* to begin each day with an official greeting. Besides, Ricky loves it, and I get a kick out of his goofy grin and the red that creeps up his neck.

My name is Magdalena Elizabeth Susannah Maria-Louise Mercer. Quite a mouthful, isn't it? Not many people know the whole thing; most just call me Maggie. My mother decided, since I was going to be an only child, to use up her entire quota of girl-names all at once. About ran out of room on my birth certificate.

I've lived in Mossy Creek for all of my forty, *ahem*, odd years. I married, had two boys, and became a widow here. Now I'm the admin-specialist and dispatcher for the local P.D.

Ricky's a big, meaty kid, not fat, just big—hefty; played fullback in high school with my oldest. I tend to treat him like my own and he's okay with that. His mom and dad and I used to see each other when we took our boys to practices, and sat next to each other at the games, screaming out our lungs for the Mossy Creek Mountain Lions.

Gage and Dawson, my birth-boys, are living (*sigh*) far away. Well, no, not *that* far away, just the next town or so over, but they're not right next door, so it seems like a long way. They come to my rescue when needed, and visit every so often ... to raid my pantry. They moved out, but I'm still feeding them. Funny how that works. And I'm not complaining. Still, it's not the same as having them home.

That's where Ricky comes in. I'm perfectly capable of performing physical labor around my own house; I'm no wimp in that department. But I like knowing there's someone I can call—someone who lives in the same neighborhood—willing and able, when necessary, to mow the lawn, rake leaves, or shovel my driveway.

You're laughing.

His parents moved to Florida last winter, so Ricky and I have developed this win-win situation. He does *chores* ... and, in return, gets baked goods, free meals, and that all-important part—fussed over.

Now stop.

He's not at my house every day, or even every week, just once in awhile. And as long as he's fed, he's more than happy to do whatever needs doing.

A boy (don't care if he's eighty, or whether he admits it or not) misses his parents, so I provide Rick that homey comfort. *Moi* yearns for her boys, and our one and only police officer is a great surrogate for the in-between times, until the originals mosey on home.

Sometimes Ricky acts the hick. But, don't let that fool you, those brain cells of his work overtime. He may have been a hotshot jock, but he'd been a member of the Honor Society all through high school. Started college in pre-law, but changed mid-stream to get a degree in business management. Still not satisfied, he applied to the police academy; graduated first in his class. YAY!

The borough council offered him Walt Prescott's job after the man had a stroke; it's been eight months.

I've already said he's big, about the same as the police chief, maybe an inch or two shorter. So far, his cuteness, and that spiffy uniform haven't attracted the right girl; but he hasn't given up hope.

Don't know what's wrong with the gals around here, but if I were fifteen, *ahem*, years younger, I'd give him a run for his money. When he grins, there's this look that flashes in his dark blue eyes where you can almost see, *way way* in the back dancing a merry jig, a mischievous imp.

He wandered over to the coffee pot and inhaled … deep. He doesn't like coffee to *drink*, just to smell.

I waited. It's usually about twenty seconds after his 'aroma fix' that he makes his move on the donut box, grabbing three before anybody else gets a chance.

"Wonder if he found Wylie James."

What? His nonchalant comment had me frowning over my reading glasses. "Why would he want to?"

"I dunno." He shrugged, but didn't turn around. "Said he needed to talk to him."

"I haven't heard anything."

By his stance, the shaking head, the huffing and chin-rubbing, I could tell he was trying to figure out what was wrong. When he turned around, the look on his face—*sooo* comical, but with a hint of panic—had me biting the inside of my cheek to keep my features straight.

"Maggie?"

"Yes, Ricky?"

"Did the Chief take the donuts?"

Expected, yes, but still, it caught me off guard. Perhaps it was the puzzlement in his voice. Good thing I hadn't taken a swallow of coffee; it would've come out m'nose.

"No," I said, once I had myself under control. "I told you, he hasn't been in yet. There are no donuts."

His eyebrows, swear to God, reached up and touched his hairline. No small feat. I say that, because he wears his blonde hair like a Marine recruiter's. Not many guys look good with it that short, but he pulls it off, with flare.

"No donuts?" He lurched forward, hands pleading. "Why not? We *always* have donuts. Police stations have donuts. Shoot, Maggie, they're my breakfast." He put his hands on his stomach, hoping to get some sympathy.

Instead, I stood—fast, with my chair shooting back and hitting the filing cabinet. Even I cringed at the noise. Now, I'm not real tall, and not very wide, but apparently, the *mere* straightening of my body was intimidating, because Ricky took two steps back, shut his mouth, then swallowed … hard.

"No," I said. "*You* always have donuts." It wasn't really all that big a deal, but I wanted him to understand where I was coming from. "No one ever says 'thank you' or donates towards the cost, but those sweet confections are always expected. Now it's none of my business if you and the Chief want to clog your arteries, but you two are going to have to start shellin' out some cash."

I sure do sound bossy, don't I?

Or, was it more of a whine?

By this time, poor Ricky was backed against the wall, gulping air like a landed fish at the bottom of a boat. "S-sorry, Maggie. I … uh, I didn't mean to make you mad. Why, um, *how* come you're buyin' 'em outta your own pocket?"

Now *my* eyebrows reached high. "What do you think I've been buying them with, my good looks?"

He opened his mouth.

Nothing came out.

I wasn't mad at him. And I could have said something … a few months earlier, just hadn't. He was the one getting dumped on because there are only three of us in the office, and the boss hadn't yet arrived. I retrieved my chair and sat. "Never mind." The aggravation wasn't worth the energy. "There's something I need you to do."

No doubt still wary of my mood, he relaxed his stance, but stayed against the wall.

"What?"

"Tomorrow's the last day of school. I'd like you to go out to the swimming hole and make sure you can still read the signs. That they're all still up. While you're at it, check out that rope and tire, too. Don't want some youngster falling on their head because the rope's rotted."

He bobbed his head. "Sure, Maggie. I can do that. Good idea." He grabbed his hat, obviously anxious to be anywhere other than here. "I'll do it right now."

—

I chuckled as he hustled out the door.

Ten minutes later, re-saturated in my novel, Chief of Police Wyatt Madison walked in.

Lisa Jackson's newest would have to wait until after work. Not much of a sacrifice, believe-you-me. Sorry, Miz Jackson.

And no, I don't usually just sit at my desk reading fiction all day. There is work to be done. Same time, not having much crime around here, it can be hard to look busy, especially at the start of the day.

The highlight of every morning, though, is not snatching moments with my latest book, but watching Wyatt walk in. He has this way of moving that … um, well, excuse me while I fan myself. Let's just say he keeps that body of his in prime condition. Oh, yes he does. And now that he's available again—for the last 17-months and twenty-five days—all the single ladies around here have even more reason to celebrate. If I have anything to say about it, though, *they're* out of luck.

It's not just the six-foot-four-inch frame of chiseled muscle that perfectly fills out his official khakis; it's all of him. His face, though classically handsome, isn't pretty. More like well-used, rugged, lived-in. The kind that would fit in well at Camelot's Round Table, alongside Sirs Percival and Lancelot.

What is it about a man who doesn't shave for a day or two, or six? And his eyes, espresso brown pools, liquid temptation. Hair a deep rich shade—like semi-sweet chocolate, smooth and shiny and satiny—gets all wavy when he forgets to visit the barber. Oh, yeah.

I like a man with hair long enough to grab. Alas, I

can only *imagine* how it feels. The opportunity to find out—that *hands on* approach—hasn't presented itself. Yet.

Then, there's those cowboy boots. You can tell they're favorites. Leather's all scuffed and creased, and with that look shoes get when they've been worn a lot: comfortable. It's hard to describe, but I think you get the idea. Haven't figured out why those things are such a turn-on.

And don't really care.

Wyatt, oblivious of his effect on the opposite sex, nonetheless makes women swoon. You should be prepared, while you're here, for an impromptu sighting. Best get a fan—one of those old fashioned ones made out of cardboard. You know, like they used to give out in church on Sundays, before air conditioning.

Oh, well, maybe you're too young to remember that.

Or, too old to admit it.

Every female this side of the county line—don't matter their age—stops wherever they are, and whatever they're doing, to sigh when Police Chief Madison's in sight.

That fan I suggested will help cool you off when he steps into your path.

This morning, without the hat to distract (he looks exceptional in that hat, too), I noticed his hair was getting that **SCRUMPTIOUS** shaggy-look. You won't hear me reminding him to make a date with Hatchet Man Jack, not with my fingers itching to run through that thick mop of dark decadence.

"Maggie." He nodded in greeting, passing my

desk on the way to the coffee pot, then stopping in front of the credenza where the machine puffed out aromatic fumes. Hands went to hips—almost identical to the way Ricky had stood and, most likely, thinking the same thing.

"Where're the donuts?"

Yup, I was right.

He turned. "Ricky get to 'em already?"

I gave him the evil eye, over the glasses I'd forgotten were propped on my nose. I hastily removed them. "Good morning, Chief Madison. There aren't any donuts." Biting my lip didn't help. The words pushed past and came out. "You don't pay me enough to waste six bucks a day for those … sweet, yummy things."

Argh! I clamped my mouth shut. It wouldn't do to piss off the boss just because I was irritated at Vicki for raising her prices.

He cocked his head. "Well, first, I don't pay you, the borough does. But, that's beside the point. You pay six for six? That's a buck a piece. Why? They're four bucks a dozen at Corsair's Market."

"No, not … well, no. Before they were a quarter each, now they're fifty-cents. And I don't even eat the blasted things." He had a point. Going to Corsair's sounded like a good idea. It would also save me from having to listen to Vicki Sporelli go on and on about what a hunk Wyatt was, and always wanting to know what he was up to.

Sometimes, when my self-esteem was low, her *interrogations* tied my belly into queasy jealous knots. But the fact that I knew that *she* knew how I got to see him all day long, while she only caught glimpses, gave me the satisfying sense of rubbing her nose in it.

Saying *neener-neener* would have done it, too, truth be known. Would have shut her up good and fast. But, not wanting to make an enemy, better to put up with the bellyaches.

"Still, that's only three dollars. How'd you figure it'd be six? And, why are you using your own money? We do have a coffee fund, you know."

I blinked. Was he *that* clueless? Honestly, sometimes…. "Really? Now, why didn't I think of that?"

Sometimes only sarcasm gets through.

He crossed his arms and poked out his lower lip. I had to bite mine. Almost made me forget why I was so irked, thinking about his soft yummy lips meeting my lips—

I mentally slurped up the drool and refocused on the conversation.

"Guess it's been a while." He nodded. "How much we got in there?" He picked up the converted coffee can and shook it.

Nada.

Nothing.

He set it down and turned back.

I shook my head, wanting to say what was really going through my mind. I didn't. "You two haven't put anything in that can for at least six months. Did you actually expect to hear something moving around in there?"

Wyatt rocked back and forth, studied his boots, then looked at me. "You mean since we used the fund to buy food for the Christmas party, you've been buying donuts and coffee with your own money?"

I sniffed and looked at the fingernails on my right hand—oh, goodness, there was a hangnail. "How else were you going to get any, Sir?"

His hands again went to his hips.

I hissed in a breath as his khaki-colored police-issue shirt stretched across his chest, straining buttons and seams, then exhaled slowly, doing my best to reign in a growl of appreciation.

Good gracious he was fine. With a capital F-I-N-E.

"Why didn't you speak up sooner?"

I stared him down, then shrugged and munched up my mouth. "Thought you'd've figured it out, by now. 'Sides, until Sporelli's raised their prices, I didn't mind. And it *is* six bucks, because now, not only are they twice as much, but Vicki doesn't let me buy less than a dozen."

"So *I* couldn't go in there and just buy, say, three donuts?"

"Right." I paused, thinking. "Well, *you* could. Cuz … you know … she's *hot* for *you*. But the rest of us peons are stuck buying twelve."

I'd never seen him blush before.

"What do you mean she's hot for me? How do you know that?"

"You make a very cute couple." Oh, ouch. I bit my tongue.

"I'm not interested in Vicki," he grumbled. "It's ridiculous, and so is the cost of their donuts. Highway robbery."

"Yeah. That's what I said." Whoa. My breath stuck in my throat. *Not*? He's *not* interested in Vicki

Sporelli? Be still, my palpitating heart.

"What'd she say to that?"

"Huh? What?" I'd lost track of the conversation. "Uh, she said that um, if I wanted to make such a fuss, I could go somewhere else." I shrugged, pretending indifference, but wanting to calm myself before I hyperventilated. "So, I just didn't get any."

Glaring, he fished out his wallet and handed me a twenty. "Here. Starting tomorrow, go to Corsair's for the donuts. I'll make sure Ricky pitches in, too."

It felt like there was a hazy bubble around my head. "Thanks." I took the bill. It was hard to concentrate on what he was saying, still unbalanced as I was about him not being interested in Vicki.

He poured a cup of coffee, added some milk from the mini fridge, and sipped. "And, Maggie?"

"Yes, Sir?"

"Next time, don't wait so long telling me about a problem."

"Yes, Sir."

He glowered past me on the way to his office.

I made a face.

"And quit with the *sir* stuff. Makes me feel old and decrepit, and I'm not."

I could attest to that.

He stopped in the doorway. "Where *is* Ricky, anyway?"

"I sent him out to the swimming hole to check on things. Tomorrow starts summer recess. I'm sure there've already been kids out there, but I'll feel better after Ricky makes sure everything's in working order."

Wyatt wandered back over to my desk, and took

another swig. I stared up at him. It made my neck ache, but I didn't care.

"Good thinking, Maggie. By the way, have you seen Wylie-James this week?"

I rolled my eyes—which is *really* hard to do when you're already overstretching. You get the picture. "It's only Monday."

"You know what I mean. Call came in early this morning from Gladys Townsend. Told me his cow was lumbering down Skunk Hollow Road. Can't seem to find the man."

"Lumbering?"

"That's the word she used."

I stopped craning my neck and began to rotate it to get the kink out. "Well, he is pretty solitary. Maybe he went off to the hills again. Did you ask Mac if he's seen him?"

"Mac's fishing out at the lake; been there a week, and won't be back for another."

"Hmm. Guess he's not feeding Wylie-James's livestock then."

"See if you can get a hold of BJ. Tell him we need to talk." He laid his hand on my shoulder and gave it a squeeze ... could have sworn it became a caress.

"Um, sure, Sir ... uh, I mean, Wyatt." I stumbled like a 16-year-old with her first mad crush.

Sometimes he just catches me unawares.

I was still stuck on the Vicki-thing. Couple months ago, I'd made a pact with myself: No more pussy-footing. Go after what you want, Maggie-Lou.

With the bakery owner on the prowl, I'd just assumed the attraction mutual.

Assumptions!

16

He was fair game.

Usually, my thing is to stay in the background and not call attention to myself. Of course, he's not the only single man in Mossy Creek, but he is the only one—after me being alone for over ten years—to snag my attention.

Now that he'd confirmed that Ms. Sporelli wasn't—and *hadn't* been—on his radar, the gloves were off.

If anybody was gonna hook 'im—if he wanted to be caught—it would be me.

Eat your heart out, Vicki Sporelli.

I'm in decent shape, and far from homely. Dawson, my youngest, says I'm the only woman my age with hair almost to the waist. In the summer, I wear it pulled back, twisted, and folded into a thick chignon. A big fancy clip, from my extensive eclectic collection, keeps it up and off my neck. There's just a sprinkling of gray—don't be laughing—with the dark brown, which tends to make it more noticeable. My green eyes get more appreciation when I'm not wearing my reading glasses, but since I can't read without them, they're on my face quite a bit.

Makeup does wonders for some, but I don't use it much. Maybe if I did, Chief Madison would take more notice ... or not. He hasn't run screaming in the other direction, but there's always that little niggle in the back of my brain that keeps hammering away at my self-esteem. Up to this point, I haven't done anything but drool discreetly in my coffee cup whenever he walks into view.

By the time I shook my head, to clear out all those fraternizational thoughts—I know, that's not a real

—

17

word, but I do like my Maggie-isms—he was back in his office.

Wyatt Madison does do an excellent job as the police chief of this small municipality, and that's not just from a prejudiced point of view. He grew up here, only a few years ahead of me in school. Left right after graduation. Did half a year of pre-law before enlisting in the Navy, back when we decided to liberate Kuwait. Went through all kinds of SP (Shore Patrol—Navy's version of military police) training. Re-upped once. After his second tour, he came home and applied for the chief's job. The borough council voted him in—unanimously—over his Uncle Mort.

The base radio, on the desk across the room, crackled. "Dispatch, I need some help out here. Chief in yet?"

I hurried over.

CHAPTER TWO

"DISPATCH. HE'S HERE. What's up?"

"Get him, Maggie."

I squinted at the black speaker-box and yelled for Wyatt. The young officer sounded irritated, and winded, and scared.

"Yeah?"

"Ricky needs to talk to you."

He came up behind me. "What's going on?"

I pointed to the radio, and backed out of the way.

He keyed the mic. "Where you at, Rick?"

"The swimming hole." His voice wobbled—not normal for him. "Chief, you need to get out here. Pronto."

Wyatt paused, a two-second beat. "What's up?"

The kid took so long to reply, I looked at Wyatt.

He was looking at me.

"It's Miranda ... Miranda Richards." Ricky cleared his throat. "She's hanging out in the middle of the creek."

"Well help her down."

"Can't." Voice tight and strained. "She's *hanging* there. Been there awhile, too, looks like. Damn. Ya need to get out here right away. I'm gonna need your help to get 'er down."

"What makes you think it's her?"

"She's the only brunette on the cheerleading squad this year."

"And what does that have to do with—"

"She's wearin' her little suit."

My legs went weak and I stumbled to my chair, numb with shock.

Miranda Richards, one of our promising young teens, honor student, prom queen, and head cheerleader. We'd gone to her graduation and commencement ceremonies, only a week ago. She'd just been by last Friday gossiping about Forsythia Morgan and the woman's infernal spying.

No, Ricky had to be mistaken.

It had to be someone else.

Please, let it be someone else.

And, poor Ricky. He'd never…. This was his first dead body.

"Wyatt, he must be frantic."

Nodding, the man cleared his throat. "Officer Anderson? How you doin'?"

There was a pause. "Shaky, Sir. Tossed my cookies, like a damn—"

"Rookie?"

"Huh, yes, Sir."

"Take some deep breaths, son … real slow. I know how it is. First couple times you're the primary on scene are the hardest. You gonna tough it out?"

"Damn straight."

Wyatt nodded. "Good. Don't touch anything. I'll be there in five."

"Roger that," came a hoarse reply. "Just hurry. I hate seein' her like this. Sure is different than on those cop shows."

I was watching Wyatt.

His hands were trembling so hard he had to set the

mic down. Then, chin on his chest, he closed his eyes. "How'm I gonna tell Mac?"

I didn't think he wanted an answer; and, in any case, I didn't have one.

He blinked and turned, as though just noticing where I was, and wondering how I'd gotten there. "Call Doc Weston. Don't use the radio unless it's an emergency." He shook his head. "Sorry, you already know that."

"Yeah, I do." I nodded. "You need to go."

Still, he hesitated. "I just can't believe—"

"Neither can I. We're in shock … all of us. It'll take time for it to sink in. But, you're the one in charge."

"In charge." Resignation laced his voice. "Huh, some leader. We should call in the county—"

"Wyatt. That can wait a bit. Right now, Ricky needs you. Miranda needs you."

He ran his fingers through his hair. "Yeah, you're right. Get Doc. He'll need to … do his thing."

"Get a move on. This is what *I* do. Go do what *you* do. The sooner you get there and take care of things, the less likely some kid's going to show up."

He did a 180 and stalked back to his office, then came out with his rig, hat, and a camera. "Hold down the fort. We'll be back as soon as possible."

"Will do." I'd been reaching for the phone, but stopped to watch him strap on his gun belt—*not* a usual occurrence. My whole body was shaky. I couldn't imagine what he was feeling. Miranda was his goddaughter.

"Tell Doc to speed for once, will ya? And thanks, Maggie … for everything." He squashed his hat on his head and went out the door.

The Suburban revved. Tires squealed and loose gravel plinked against the windows as he tore out of the parking lot.

I called Doc Weston and told him where to meet Wyatt.

While waiting for them to get back, I put a call through to BJ Knowles, Wylie-James's grandson, to let him know the chief wanted a sit-down.

We'd probably have to call in the county sheriff, or the state boys, or both, but I'd leave that for Wyatt.

Where was my best friend when I needed her most? Never had I ever wanted to talk to Dandy more than I did right now. Unfortunately, Dandelion Jones, her hubby Ed, and their 10 year old son Joshua, left two days ago for a three week tour of Europe. No way would I mess up her lovely vacation with news of such tragedy. She'd be mad about that when she got back, but it was better this way.

CHAPTER THREE
TUESDAY....

NOBODY GOT TO swing off the rope at the Mossy Creek swimming hole yesterday, weren't going to today, either. The State cops had cordoned off the area, which, of course, automatically enlarged the crowd of morbid curiosity gawkers wanting to know: *What's going on? Who's under the tarp?*

Wyatt and Ricky were out there again, scouring the scene for clues. Later, they'd be talking to Miranda's friends and family, and everyone else in her circle. It had only been about twenty-four hours since she'd been discovered; they hadn't found much.

Cause of death *looked* like suicide. Wyatt said he had a hunch it wasn't that simple, but would wait on word from Harrison McCabe, the Greene County Coroner, to verify his suspicions.

Although relegated to the command post, I was itching to explore the site. Crime novels are a passion. Having read more than my share, I was sure I could find something everyone else had missed. Alas, despite wishful thinking, I wasn't allowed; didn't have a badge.

At noon, Wyatt and Ricky trudged through the door, frustration and exhaustion evident on their faces. Ricky tossed his hat on his desk; Wyatt hooked his on the back of a chair and ran his hands through the mass of sweat-dampened locks above his brow, leaving it … mussed.

(*Sigh*.) Now was not the time to drool, but there's no stopping hormones when they're agitated.

Both men sagged into the nearest seats, in front of my desk.

"Would you like some lunch?" They had to be hungry. Whether they were or not, they needed to eat. "I could call over to Annetta's and have something delivered?"

Wyatt had a weakness for her special hoagies.

"Sounds great, Maggie." His unenthused answer made me frown.

"Ricky?"

"Sure … yeah, whatever."

"What do you want them to bring?"

Leaning forward in his chair, Wyatt rubbed his hands over his face before letting them hang between his knees. "I don't even have an appetite."

"You have to eat." I sounded like my mother.

Don't think he noticed. "Yeah, I know. All right, well, one of her hot ham and cheese hoagies, I guess. And a Pepsi … two-liter."

I waited a few seconds. "Pie?"

His eyes met mine. A brief grin appeared and was gone. "Sure. Coconut cream."

"Rick, how about you?" Pen stood poised. "I feel like one of her waitresses."

The boy slid his frame down far enough to rest his head against the chair's back, stretched out his legs, then crossed his ankles. "Sounds good. What Wyatt ordered. 'Cept no coconut; make mine banana."

"All right. Two hot ham and cheeses, with Pepsi's, one coconut cream and one banana."

Wyatt rifled through his billfold and handed me a couple of tens. "Get something for yourself, too. On second thought, why don't you go pick it up? Get out of here for a few. You've been manning your post since all this started, practically without a break."

It made me feel good, him noticing. He and Ricky had been just as diligent, more so even; but I wasn't above accepting lavish praise upon occasion.

Ricky sat up long enough to get out his wallet. "Ten be enough?" He passed it over, then slouched down, closing his eyes.

"It'll be plenty, thanks. I'll be right back. You two go take a nap."

With Annetta's only two blocks down the street, there was no need to drive. It would take longer to find a parking space than to walk. Minutes later, there, and buried within a crowd—everyone liked to eat at Annetta's—I was immediately accosted by the local Clark Kent wanna-be, Daniel Harris.

"Mags, what's the latest?"

He was also the only one in town with the audacity to call me that idiotic nickname.

"Clark," I retaliated. "No comment."

I made my way to the take-out counter.

He followed, like a puppy wanting scraps. "Aw, c'mon. You know everything that's happening. The people have a right to know!"

I swiveled. "What about the victim's right to privacy!"

He shrugged. "She's dead. What does she care?"

I blinked, shocked and disgusted. "I can't believe you're that callous. She was one of us. She's got a father, remember?" I couldn't believe it, the *man* wasn't even offended. "Have a heart, why don't ya?"

"He's still out on the lake." Daniel smiled. "He doesn't even know."

I lifted my chin. "I give up."

He leaned closer, smelling a possible tidbit. "Are you saying he's been notified?"

"I'm not confirming or denying. But—and be sure to put this one in big quotes [a finger thumps Daniel's forehead] up in your brain—if I read one single word of this conversation in the paper, your father will be hearing about it."

He narrowed his eyes, and tried one last time. "Mags, you're the only one who can tell us anything."

"First of all, if I said anything, even *off* the record—which you have no clue about—I'd be fired; then, of course, I'd have to hurt you. Secondly, if I told everything I knew, about *everyone* in this town, I'd have a bestseller. And the stuff about *you*, dear boy, would be the juiciest."

He blushed—he really did—and stammered a little as he backed away, tucking his notepad into a shirt pocket. Funny how I seem to have that effect on younger men.

"You haven't been a saint yourself, ya know."

"Never said I was. Now, leave me alone. I need to order. Annetta?"

The woman came up to the register, trying to hide a grin. "Take out?"

"Yes, please." I gave her the order, adding a hot turkey and cheddar for myself.

"Coming right up. Wait. Only two desserts?" As I nodded, she stuck the pencil over her ear and walked back toward the kitchen. "Gobbler with CHEESE."

She opened the dessert case. "AND TWO PIG MELTS—lickety-split!"

Thirty minutes later, back at headquarters, the dynamic duo and I were enjoying lunch.

"By the way, standing in line at Annetta's, I got waylaid by that jerk—"

"Oh, yeah?" Wyatt leaned forward.

"Don't worry, I handled it. Danny Harris, being his usual obnoxious self, intimated that Mac was still up at the lake, and tried grilling me for info. About Mac, you bring him back yesterday, right?"

"I did," Wyatt said. "Danny thinking he's privy to everything that goes on in this town is *his* fantasy. Most of the time, it's all guesswork. Only way he gets his story is when people verify or deny."

"Well, he didn't get anything from me." I wrinkled my nose. "At least, I don't think he did. I also let him know what would happen if our conversation ever made the paper."

Ricky laughed. "What'd you threaten him with?"

"His father, I'll betcha," Wyatt interrupted, laughing.

I smacked his shoulder. "How'd you know?"

Ricky answered for him. "Because, Maggie, we both had dads!"

I should've known. Of course, Ricky was right, and with Daniel Harris, his father was one tough hombre. Owen Harris not only owned the local rag, but knew he was part of the town as much as anyone else, and on his worst day wouldn't allow anybody in Mossy Creek to get disparaged just for the sake of a story, and certainly not by his newshound of a son.

Although it didn't have a big circulation, *The*

Mossy Creek Gazette was the town's only printed source of information. The death of Miranda Richards had made the front-page, and everyone was hungry for more details, especially the police department—both of them, maybe-sorta three of 'em.

"What about a press conference?" Ricky shoveled a bite of banana cream pie into his mouth.

Wyatt waved in dismissal. "What can we tell them that they don't already know? Officer Anderson found Miranda Richards hanging from a rope at the swimming hole? Most likely cause of death? Suicide. Yeah right, maybe." He shook his head. "The earliest we can confirm that will be the end of the week, with the coroner's report."

He picked up his sandwich. "What else? That friends say she was at an end-of-year pep rally at the high school Friday afternoon, but no one saw her after that? Her dad didn't report her missing, because he's been out at Grand View Lake on a fishing trip? I mean, hell, that's it, end-of-report."

He shifted to get a two-handed grip on the last quarter of his hoagie. "Now, we could ask for everyone's help, in case they have any other information, but I gotta say, I think we've about tapped that source. And, as I said before, and just for our ears, it might *look* like suicide, but I wouldn't bet on it." A glance at Ricky. "Wasn't she going out with Dodge Peters's kid? What's his name?"

Ricky finished a swallow of Pepsi, belched, then answered, "'Scuse me. No, it wasn't the Peters's kid. It was the Reverend's," a cough, "Reverend Blanchard's kid, Eddy."

"Oh?" I pursed my lips. "I could've sworn

Forsythia Morgan told me she saw Cody Peters and Miranda holding hands at the carnival last week."

Ricky and Wyatt stopped chewing and looked at each other.

I quirked my eyebrows. "What?"

"At the same carnival, yeah. BJ Knowles said he saw her with ol' Danny-boy."

"Him, too? Wow! Girl got around."

"Miranda was out with Daniel 'Clark Kent' Harris? *Eeeuw*." The thought ruined my appetite. I picked up my sandwich, balanced my elbows on the desk. "Hopefully, it was on a different night." Taking a bite, but noticing the other two staring, I made sure to swallow my mouthful before saying anything else. "Oh, *puh-leease* … you can't tell me, while you're in high school and not going steady, that there's something wrong with dating more than one guy at a time?"

Wyatt cleared his throat. "No. There's nothing wrong with it. Except the girls on Miranda's cheerleading squad let it slip that *Randy* was real excited about some 'secret' guy she'd met back in March. Seems they'd been meeting behind-the-bush because of his age. So, technically, I guess you could say she *was* going steady with someone."

"I know I'd be pissed if *my* girl was hanging out at the carnival with two or three different guys." Ricky took another swig of Pepsi. "Think maybe her mystery man found out and blew a gasket?"

"Possibly." Wyatt propped his feet on the corner of the desk. "We already know her neck was broken from Doc Weston's initial exam. The coroner's report will tell us what really happened."

"Could be the guy threatened her and ... and she couldn't deal with it. But ... man ... hanging's a bad way to die—or so I've been told. And it sure is ugly to find somebody that way; not like it is in the movies." Ricky got up and threw his trash in the bin. "I can't believe a high school senior would commit suicide a week or so after graduation."

"Neither can I; especially not my goddaughter. Which is why I don't think it was suicide. The way you found her, though," Wyatt shook his head. "She could *not* have been dead before getting tangled in that rope. Her body position was consistent with a hanging, but what if she was semi-conscious, or drugged when someone wrapped that cord around her neck and dropped her from the branch?"

I grimaced at the vision, feeling a little queasy. "She could have ... um, *un*-raveled before it went taut."

Wyatt nodded. "True enough. Let's assume she was unconscious."

"The word is *presumed*."

Wyatt looked over. "What's that, Maggie?"

"Sorry. To quote my favorite English teacher: 'One *assumes* a title, position, or responsibility ... but when a dunderhead's guessing, he's *pre*suming.' Guess I never got it out of my head. Continue, please."

"Lesson learned, Maggie, thanks. Anyway, someone with a lot of upper-body strength could lower her from the branch. The constriction wouldn't be sudden or risky, so there'd be no way for her to buck loose."

Ricky, looking gecko around the gills, agreed.

30

"Yeah. That sounds likely. I mean, if she just dropped, or *got* dropped, she'd have lost at least a shoe, right? I mean they were untied, but still on her feet."

"Now there's a clue nobody mentioned before." I grabbed a steno book and pen. "Did Miranda's friends have any idea who this secret paramour was?"

Two puzzled pairs of eyes. "Paramour?"

Ah, MEN. "You know, a leading man, beau, lover, a Don Juan, a friggin' stud."

Wyatt laughed. "You don't read just murder mysteries, do you, Maggie?"

I slapped a thigh and grinned. "Did they?"

Silence.

"The question, remember? You'd asked about Miranda's friends?"

Ricky shook his head, his lips quirking with amusement. "Nope, just that he was older."

"Hmm." A finger drum. "I wonder if she kept a diary. Have you searched Mac's place yet? We should make sure to look for one."

Wyatt looked over. "We?"

Oops.

"Sorry. I keep forgetting I'm not *oh*-fficially on the force."

He chuckled. "Don't worry about it. Even though it's my case, the County boys did an initial search before I brought Mac back, then the staties went through. I'll buzz him, and say…" He stopped and stared, probably to make sure I was looking at him (I was, of course). "…that we'll be coming over."

My cheeks burned. "Thank you. I'd love to go."

Laughter.

31

"Maggie, you've been reading way too many mysteries."

"Actually, not enough, Ricky." No shame to admit it. "Blame *Malone*, *Remington Steele*, and the great Sam Spade."

"Blame 'em? I'm ready to thank 'em." Wyatt winked. "I'll be in my office giving Mac a call, let 'im know what time to expect us."

"That'd be great."

"Ricky, what's on your agenda?"

"Going back to the school. There's a faculty meeting this afternoon—secretary's told them to wait for me."

"What about her cheerleading coach?" I began to clean the lunch mess from my desk. "They can be trustworthy confidants. Maybe Miranda talked to her."

"She's on my list. She was gone when I was there this morning, had a dentist appointment. May or may not yet be back." Ricky walked to the door, hat in hand. "I'll check in with y'all when I'm through."

CHAPTER FOUR

SETTLED AT MY DESK, it was time to make a list. I wasn't sure what all to write, but figured I'd have to incorporate everything I found out, along with whatever Wyatt and Ricky gleaned from their interviews. Right now, though, it was a very short list.

I was still doodling when the front door opened and a man came in. A man in a courier's uniform. My glasses came off. "Hi. Can I help you?"

He was cute in a breathless, red-faced, sweaty sort of way.

"Urgent delivery for Chief of Police Wyatt Madison, from the Greene County Coroner. Is he in?"

"What'd you do, run all the way over here from the county seat?"

Grinning, he shook his head. "Bicycle. Training for the Summer Solstice Race."

"That's a long trek. How cool is that? Want some water?" Very impressive. Seventeen miles, one way, on a bike, is nothing to sneeze at. He didn't seem to need much training. His buns and thighs were perfectly compact and—

"No thanks. I've got a bottle on my bike."

I sat up a little straighter, suddenly remembering his query. "The Chief's in his office. Hang on, I'll get him."

I knocked on Wyatt's door.

"Yeah?"

I poked my head inside. He was on the phone,

size twelve's propped on the desk. I whispered, loudly. "We got a courier."

Nothing.

Louder, "Wyatt, we got a courier—from county!"

His feet hit the floor. "Call you back, Mac." He stood. "Where is he?"

"At my desk. Should I send him in, or you coming out?"

He was already on the move. "Out."

Just as the courier was handing over the envelope to Wyatt, the phone rang. "Mossy Creek Police Department. How may I help you?"

I can be very professional when the mood hits.

Harrison McCabe for Police Chief Madison. Report get there, yet?"

"Yes, Sir, just now."

"Great. Wyatt there?"

"Yes, Sir. Just a moment." Phone's passed to Wyatt. "Greene County Coroner."

"Harry? What can I do for you?"

I watched as his face went a little gray.

The conversation was all one-sided, except for an occasional grunt or sigh from Wyatt that seemed to go on, for so long that by the time he hung up, I was ready to bite my fingernails.

Then, leaving me exasperated with curiosity, he walked over to Mr. Buns, signed the release, and shook the man's hand. The cyclist nodded to me, donned his helmet and left the building.

"Wyatt—"

"Maggie," he interrupted before I could even ask my question, "Doc says not to 'sir' him anymore."

"Okay." I squinted. "Wyatt—"

He held up a hand. "My office."

My mouth snapped shut and my eyebrows came together, but I silently followed, toward the inner sanctum.

He stopped and turned so fast I ran into him. His elbow connected with my chin. Stars danced as my teeth clacked together. A sharp groan of pain slid out and I stumbled sideways, holding my jaw.

"MAGGIE, damn, I'm so sorry." Hands reached to steady me. "Can you find Ricky and get him here, ASAP? Better yet, why don't you wait at your desk 'til he gets here? Then I won't have to tell it twice." He made sure I had my feet under me before letting go of my arms.

I was tempted to pretend, so he'd have to help me to my chair, but he was so ... out of sorts, I decided to forego the flirtatiousness. Dr. McCabe had obviously delivered some devastating news.

My frown deepened. Worried, and massaging my still-smarting face, I went back to my desk. I'd never seen him this upset. The coroner's verbal report must have been worse than expected, and he hadn't even read the written one, yet. I chewed my bottom lip a while, mulling it over. Then I remembered he wanted me to call Ricky. *Shoot*. I went to the radio, muttering.

Ricky didn't answer. I crossed my arms and glared at the mic. Another five minutes, and I'd try again.

I didn't have to wait that long.

"Dispatch, Officer Anderson here." The voice boomed out of the speaker.

Cringing at the blast of sound, I lowered the

---

volume, and keyed the mic. "Go ahead, Rick."

"Hey, Maggie. I just finished talking to a couple of her teachers, and the cheerleading coach. Hey, did you know Lancy Farnsworth's running the squad? I went to school with her."

"Nope. Wasn't aware of that."

"She sure is cute. Hell, she could pass as one of her girls."

"That's no surprise, you haven't been out of school that long, Rick. You should ask her out."

A pause.

Maybe I'd embarrassed him.

"Um, I did find out some other stuff … *interesting* stuff." He didn't go into detail, which was a good thing. Anyone with a scanner now had it tuned in to our frequency.

"Chief's got some, too. Disturbing. Wants a powwow, ASAP."

"Roger, that. Be there in … about ten minutes."

"Good. He seems …," I struggled to find the right word, "… grave."

"Grave?"

"Yeah. That's the word. Grave."

A longer pause this time, as though he needed a moment for the words to sink in. "I'll hurry."

"Roger. Out."

Fifteen minutes later, Ricky and I slipped into Wyatt's office, quiet as … on tiptoe. We glanced at each other, then at him, as we took our seats. He sat behind his desk, elbows leaned on the top, hands over his face.

"Boss?" Ricky's voice was low.

With a deep sigh, that I swear might have hidden a sob, Wyatt raised his head. What a shock. Red eyes and a ravaged look told me the man was deep in grief.

He cleared his throat, and folded his arms. "I just heard from the county coroner, and read his report. It makes me—" He shook his head. "I can't even describe. I was right, though. My goddaughter didn't commit suicide."

I blinked, not surprised, but shocked all the same. Someone, in our quiet little borough, had killed one of our children. One member of our close-knit community was a monster.

We'd thought of it before, but now, from a different angle, it was more real … more chilling. Which one of our townsfolk could have done something so horrific?

"That's not all, is it?"

"No." There was a long pause. "Said it looked like someone first bashed her in the head, which may have knocked her out. Killer probably thought she was dead. Then strangled her as she regained consciousness. Harry says the hanging could have been to cover up the finger marks around her throat. His findings indicate she was alive when the rope went around her neck, but he's relatively sure she was unconscious. Thank God for something."

Ricky shuddered. "It makes my stomach jump to think about. All I can see is my sister strung up like that, trying to get loose. Yeah, she's older than

Miranda, but … man. I hope t'God she didn't know what was happening." He blew out a sharp breath and rubbed his face. "Murder just doesn't happen around here. Why now? Why her? And who the hell could have done it … would have the balls to do it?"

I looked at Wyatt, bottom lip between my teeth. "What else?" I didn't want to hear anymore, but he wasn't through. From the look on his face, whatever was next was more than bad.

"She was pregnant … three months along."

Much worse.

I sniffled, as tears welled, and spilled. We couldn't have imagined that possibility. "Oh, Wyatt. Have you told Mac?"

"No. I wanted y'all up to speed first. I'm gonna head out to his place when we're done here. It's gonna take a while, and he's gonna need a lot of support after." He looked at Ricky, then me. "I know you're anxious to get that search done and over with, but, personally, I want to give Mac a little time to absorb this latest news. Yes, it's a murder investigation. Yes, we need to be gung-ho to find the killer. Yes, we're law enforcement and should be tougher … meaner … colder, than this." He leaned back in his chair. "I just can't do that to him. This is a major emotional hit for *me*; but it will *shatter* him. He needs to— I don't know how much more he can deal with, right now. Tomorrow will be soon enough to make the search."

"Before you leave, Ricky had some news." I nodded over at the big boy … sorry, young man. My oldest is still a boy to me, and he's the same age.

Ricky looked as devastated as Wyatt. I was, too,

but it seemed harder to see it on their faces than feel it in my heart.

"This seems inconsequential, especially after what we just heard." Ricky wiped his eyes, took out his little notebook, and coughed a couple times to get the gravel out of his voice. "I still have a few teachers to catch up with, but I got the best lead so far from Lancy. She's the cheerleading coach. Told me Miranda Richards was the exclusive babysitter for the mayor and his wife."

My eyebrows rose. "Well, you don't say? How very interesting." I twiddled my pen between my fingers. "But, I'm not exactly sure why, just yet."

Ricky sighed, shaking his head. "You been watchin' Forensic Files again, Maggie?"

CHAPTER FIVE

WEDNESDAY....

ROUND ABOUT NINE a.m., the front door opened. I was typing up a vandalism report that had mysteriously appeared in my IN box. Yes, I *do* perform police-related work from time to time. My concentration went out the window, though, as Vera-Mae Wellington limped, with dignity, into the room. She didn't usually venture out of her house, let alone come into town, which is why seeing her was such a shock.

She shuffled her ultra slim five-foot-nothing person toward my desk with the help of a large wooden cane. A big, bulky, tan elastic-wrap covered her left leg from the ankle, all the way up underneath her calf-length, purple paisley shirtdress. "Magdalena." She nodded in greeting. "Very nice to see you, dear."

Her speech was just shy of slurred, as if her dentures were loose. She wore a faded purple-felt pillbox hat on her short snow-white hair, and white cotton gloves. A square, white-plastic pocketbook hung stiff from her right arm. She looked like she'd just stepped out of a 1950's best-dressed poster.

"Miz Wellington, what brings you in to see us today?"

I moved around my desk to pull a chair out for her.

She settled in, crossing her ankles awkwardly—because of the bandage—and holding onto her handbag like it was a lifeline. "Well, now, I just had to come in, because, as you know, I don't have a telephone."

I nodded. "Yes, Ma'am, I *do* know. And the chief is very concerned about you living so far away from folks, and not having a way to contact anyone, in case something—God forbid—should ever happen."

"I don't think it would make much difference if I had a telephone or not. If I were to fall down the stairs, how-*ever* would I reach the thing?" She fiddled with her gloves. "Besides, I've been thinking … still of two minds about it. My family does visit quite often … sometimes too often. Cain't nevah—" She stopped, and attempted to compose herself. "I apologize. Sometimes it's hard to get rid of them, and gets quite annoying. I enjoy being alone, and it is usually quiet out my way. That's one of the reasons I'm here."

"It isn't quiet, anymore?"

She nodded, the slightest inclination. "I need to make a report. May I give it to you?"

"Yes, Ma'am. Just let me get my Steno and we'll get started." I opened the middle drawer of my desk and retrieved my case book. After finding a clean page, and with pen poised, I said, "All right, Miz Wellington, what is the nature of your report?" I figured she was going to tell me about a stray cat, or maybe a mangled postal box via teens playing mailbox baseball.

Boy, was I wrong.

"Well you see, the other night I was sitting out on

41

my back porch enjoying a nice mint julep."

I raised my eyebrows at that, but kept writing, without comment. Our Miss (Prissy Spinster) Wellington drinking mint juleps, all alone, and getting a little loopy was too outrageous to fathom. Could it be?

"A car pulled up to the swimming hole."

Sorry, I suppose I ought to have mentioned earlier that her property buttresses against the creek near the swimming hole.

"What night was this, Miz Wellington?"

She held a gloved hand against her chest. "Oh, let's see, I believe it was Friday, or perhaps, Saturday evening."

"And this particular car caught your attention, because…?" I dangled that … er, question, not giving a thought to whom I was speaking.

She gave me a look I hadn't seen since Granny Ellis caught me getting my lips taste-tested by my first boyfriend. "My dear, Magdalena," she sighed. "Didn't I teach you English any better than that? You should have asked, 'Why was this car more unusual than most?'"

"I apologize, Miz Wellington." And I was truly sorry. I *did* know better than that. And, before you ask, yes, she was my tenth-grade English teacher, back when they called it English … not Communications Art or Language Arts, or some other such nonsense. "Why was this car more unusual than most?"

Mollified, she relaxed a bit in the chair. "Well, I didn't think it was, until I noticed that cheerleader getting out of it."

—

She'd caught my attention. "Cheerleader? You saw Randy ... er, Miranda Richards? Did you see who she, uh ... who was with her?"

The hat never moved as she shook her head, although her hair did get slightly mussed. "I heard her laugh at something. She was with a man, because I heard his voice, too. Um, to be precise, I heard a deeper voice and presumed it to be a man. But, I couldn't see clearly enough through my lilac bushes to recognize anyone." Her mouth set in disgust; she paused and *tsk*-ed.

"The only reason I know she was a cheerleader, is because of the uniform ... the one with the cute little red skirt. I did think it odd, at the time. She should not have been wearing her costume. It just didn't seem appropriate." Miz Wellington began to wring her hands.

"They weren't there very long. I'd guess it was about twenty minutes or so when they came back to the car. She sounded upset. His voice was tense, like a scolding parent. I couldn't make out any of the words, just the sounds of their voices. They got back into the car and she spun the tires in the gravel on the way out."

"Did you see what kind of car it was?"

"Miranda's little blue Datsun."

"So, *she* was driving." It wasn't a question.

"Yes, I believe I said that already."

"So you did." I sat back in my chair. "Miz Wellington, didn't Chief Madison or Officer Anderson come by to talk to you?"

She tilted her head in thought. "No. I don't believe so. Unless I was napping. I take out my hearing aids when I lay down. However, I may not have gotten home yet."

"Home from where?"

She made an impatient sound. "One thing at a time, dear."

I was getting edgy and mentally forced myself to relax. "What time of day was this?"

"Oh, in the evening, dear. I'd say probably seven-thirty, eight … something like that. Not completely dark, but not real light."

"Twilight?"

"Mmm, yes. Twilight. A perfect description."

"Thank you so much, Miz Wellington. I'll be sure to tell the chief when he gets back." I stood, about to help her out of the chair.

She tilted forward a little and placed a gloved hand on the edge of my desk. "Oh, that's not all."

CHAPTER SIX

"NOT ALL?" I raised my eyebrows and sat back down. "What else?"

I should have been paying better attention.

She relaxed again. "Well now, I told you I take out my hearing aids when I lie down." I nodded. "I went to bed, around eleven-thirty." She stopped, put her forefinger over her mouth, thought for a moment, then directed it at me. "You know I do believe it was Sunday evening. Yes. Yes, it was, because after I went inside, I turned on the television and watched the Sunday night movie on ABC, then the news at eleven, before I went up to bed.

"I mentioned that her attire puzzled me, did I not?"

I smiled, and flipped back a few pages. "Yes, you are correct, Miz Wellington. You did say it was odd, and seemed inappropriate."

She inclined her head. "She shouldn't have been wearing it, because there aren't any high school sports on Sundays. Just now, in speaking of it, I realize she had just graduated; therefore, technically, she was no longer a cheerleader.

"I'm still not sure what woke me, but lights flashed across my wall and I got up to look out the window. It was very dark by that time. I could see taillights and headlights." She shifted in her seat, as though anxious. "Someone got out of the car, because a dome light blinked on-and-off. It came on again, and I saw him lean in and wrestle something— obviously heavy—from the front passenger seat. I didn't realize what it was until he walked in front of the car and was momentarily highlighted. He was carrying a girl ... I could see her bare legs swinging." Both hands went to her chest this time, and she leaned forward.

"That's when I wished, with all my heart, that I had a telephone. I couldn't very well go anywhere in my car, as I don't know where the Chief Madison lives. Also, because my doctor won't allow me to drive after dark anymore. I thought about running out to the swimming hole, but I didn't know who was out there, or what they were doing, (she cupped a hand to her mouth) it could have been a romantic tryst. I never imagined—"

She paused, to recompose.

"I suppose it was about ten or fifteen minutes later—more or less, I can't be certain—when I saw him come back alone. He then got into the car and drove away."

"You believe the person you saw was male?"

"No. I couldn't tell either way. It's just a pronoun specification."

"Why didn't you come to see us the next day?"

"I'm getting to that," she snapped. "The next morning, I got up and had every intention of coming in to see Chief Madison. But it just so happened that my sister's girl Bernice was coming by to take me to the grocer's. Corsair's was having a sale on chicken, and it's always so much fresher and well-cleaned than— *Ahem*. As I was saying, I was combing my hair and heard the car in the drive."

She shook her head. "In my haste to get to the door, I stumbled on the stairs, and fell. I couldn't move for a few minutes, but my lungs worked just fine. Bernice used her key to get in. I didn't think I was hurt all that badly, but when I tried to stand, my leg wouldn't hold." She paused to massage said leg. "Thankfully she's stronger than she looks and we made it out to her car and went to the emergency room over to Arlington." With an irritated huff, she said, "Blasted know-it-alls. They took X-rays of everything and found that though nothing was broken, I had badly sprained my knee, possibly even my hip. Because of my age, the doctor … young whippersnapper, decided to keep me for observation, in case I developed any delayed reactions. Such twaddle. I should have beaned him with my cane, except I didn't have one at the time."

I bit my lip to keep a straight face.

"Needless to say, I was very put out and not able to come forward about what I'd seen. Upon arriving home, I learned about that poor little girl—and *that* [her hand slaps the table] very night, too—dying out at the swimming hole. I was beside myself, wondering, if I *had* been able to call someone, if she might still be alive.

"I had to wait until today, when Bernice came by to check on me. So, here I am, and have told you as much as can be remembered."

My head was spinning, and I had writer's cramp from all the new information she'd recounted. "Miz Wellington, you saw the same man twice?"

She shook her head. "No, I can't say that—and I

won't. Now that I think on it, the shape was different the second time. But, as I said before, it was very late by then, and I'd been asleep."

"Was it Miranda's car, or a different one?"

She pursed her lips in thought. "It could have been, but it was dark. I can't be certain."

"You're sure you couldn't tell who it was?"

She fisted her hands around the handle of her pocketbook. "I've been wracking my brain since it happened. The build was familiar, but with the distance and the lack of light—well, as I said before, I can't even say for certain it was the same person both times."

I closed my Steno. "Thank you so much for coming in. The information you've given will be immensely helpful. Can you think of anything you'd like to add?"

"No. I believe that's all there is."

"Once Chief Madison reads this, I'm sure he'll want to talk to you."

"Oh." Pink bloomed on her cheeks, but she protested. "That won't be necessary. I wouldn't want to waste his time."

"It wouldn't be a waste, Miz Wellington." I shrugged. "It's possible that once you get home, something new will come to mind. Or, he may ask you questions I didn't, and it'll jog a memory."

With a sigh, she capitulated. "If he's that determined, I suppose I can't stop him." A hand cupped to her mouth again. "And perhaps I shouldn't want to."

Laughter from us both.

"I'm sure, once I give him your report, he'll make

it a point to come by for a visit."

Her blush deepened. She smiled and stood without my help. "Well then," she gave a cutesy-girl shrug and a giggle. "I'll have to make a fresh batch of mint juleps."

I swallowed a laugh, but let loose my grin.

Her smile widened. "He is quite dishy, if you ask me."

"Oh, I do agree with you there, Miz Wellington. One hundred percent."

I got up and offered her the crook of my elbow.

"Thank you, dear." She patted my arm before clasping it. "You know, I very much enjoyed having you in class, Magdalena. You were one of my favorite students. I was very sorry to hear of your loss."

Well, gee, what can you say back to that? "Thank you, Miz Wellington. I enjoyed *being* in your class, too. You learned me a lot."

She slapped my arm with her pocketbook.

Seriously, I *had* enjoyed her class.

I held the door and noticed Bernice coming up the stone steps. We nodded greetings, and I handed Miz Wellington over to her care. Back inside, I made a beeline for the dispatch radio and called Wyatt.

Boy, did I have some info for him.

It wasn't but about ten minutes after Vera-Mae left that Forsythia Morgan popped in. Now, Forsythia is a Mossy Creek rumor mill specialist, and by that, I mean she's a busybody … a vicious gossip.

The grapevine is faster than the speed of light, and she has a lot to do with that. You could even go so far as to say, she's the unofficial president. She and Carly Prescott—God rest her *spiteful* soul—started things off back when there were still party-line telephones.

If Forsythia sees your shades go down a minute too early on a Saturday night, she's on the phone spreading the word that you've got company. She stirred up Reverend Blanchard's congregation that way. Told anyone who'd listen: *'that hypocritical man of God was 'playing footsy' with Betsy Peters'*— Dodge's wife.

Turns out, Mrs. Bladdermouth ended up with yolk all over her face, because Betsy was helping the Reverend plan the annual Summer Fair. Mrs. Blanchard—God rest her saintly soul—had been diagnosed with breast cancer and was undergoing treatments. There was no way the frail woman was in any shape to handle the details of putting together a fair, especially one that size.

Forsythia apologized in front of the congregation and everything, but it didn't stop her from gossiping.

Now, she was here on my turf. I didn't figure I'd have to wait long to find out what she wanted, and that I wasn't going to like it.

"Magdalena," she gushed at me, smiling … largely. "How are you, dear? And your boys?"

"Just fine, Miz Morgan. How're you?" I shuffled papers on my desk to hide the notes from Vera-Mae's visit.

"Oh, just dandy, thank you. Yes. Um, I couldn't

help but notice, my good friend Vera-Mae was just in for a visit. Might unusual, hmm?"

I stuck my tongue between my teeth and clamped down—not too hard, though—just enough to stop the urge to—

I nodded.

She smiled, a hard stretch of her mouth. "She was wearing a pretty big bandage on her leg."

I nodded, again.

Her face began to lose its friendly façade. "Um, did she happen to mention how she came to be wearing it?"

I nodded once more, wondering why she didn't ask the woman herself, since they were such *good* friends. I kept my mouth shut, not about to open that can of worms.

"Magdalena." Her tone screamed exasperation, but she was too stubborn to make a fuss. "Magdalena," she said again, after a long pause. Then came that famous nasty undertone. "Did you know she im-bibes?"

I canted my head to the right and mouthed the word *really*.

"Yes, indeed." She puffed up her chest. "She gets downright soused, let me tell you. Her and those mint juleps she makes. Why, those things are lethal. Doesn't take but two to make her ... well ... tipsy."

I couldn't help myself. "So, you've had a sample?"

Her jaw dropped, but she quickly closed it. Now, I could tell she was in a quandary. If she said yes, I'd know she was just as guilty. If she said no, I could accuse her of maligning the good name and character of a popular former schoolteacher. With a pinch to her lips and a glare in her eyes, she asked, "Is the chief in?"

"No, Ma'am. He is not. Would you like to leave a message?"

She hesitated. "Yes. Tell him I would like to speak to him about the shameful suicide of Miranda Richards."

"Oh, you mean the Chief's goddaughter?" Anger burned in my belly. *Self-righteous old biddy.* I had to bite my tongue a little harder, to *not* say it out loud. I scribbled some lines on a piece of paper. "I'll leave a note on his desk."

Forsythia turned pure tomato. "Well ... don't be too fast with that; after all, young lady, we must allow the Chief his time of mourning. I just wanted to let *you* know."

"Of course, what was I thinking." I tore the note up.

She nodded, stiff and ultra-polite. "Thank you, Magdalena. Good day."

"Good day."

As soon as the door shut behind her, I growled.

I had just settled down from Forsythia's visit, when BJ Knowles walked in. Of course, I've already mentioned that BJ is Wylie-James's grandson.

A nice kid, beanpole skinny and tall, exactly like Wylie-James. His hair's a scruffy dirty-blonde that needed to see a barber, and he had the bluest eyes I've ever seen. When he smiled, his whole face lit up.

He was a suspect, of sorts, since folks had seen him in the company of Miranda Richards before her death. He wasn't here about that, though; he was here about his grandfather's livestock, or at least, one particular wandering cow.

Wyatt had asked BJ to have a look-see to find out what was going on with the animals at his grandfather's property.

"Hey, Miz Mercer." His greeting was as formal as it gets around here.

"BJ. What can I do for you?"

"Chief Madison asked me to meet him here."

"That's fine. Have a seat. He's not back yet."

"Thanks." He went to sit on the bench along the wall on the other side of my desk.

"Did you get your grandfather's cow back to pasture?"

He gave a laugh. "Yeah, but I had to fix the fence first." He frowned. "You know, looked like somebody'd run into it. But, everybody's where they belong, again, and I fed 'em all while I was out there. Wish I knew where he'd got to. Momma's all worked up about it." He looked down at his hands. "Me, too."

I sympathized. "He's got everyone worked up, BJ. Everybody likes your granddad."

"Yeah."

Wyatt came in. "BJ, good of you to stop by. Come on back to my office." He winked at me on his way past my desk. Flustered the vinegar right out of me. I think I might have blushed, but then had to frown. He'd done that on purpose, so I'd be distracted and wouldn't be curious enough to follow him and BJ.

UGH!

I shook my head free of those bad thoughts. Maybe he wasn't being sneaky, just flirty … which was more enjoyable than an upfront approach. I couldn't fault him for that; I liked to do it, too.

I hunted through my pile for the notes I'd hidden from Forsythia. With Wyatt busy until BJ left, I might as well type them up. Ricky was due in any minute, and unless Wyatt had another interview, the three of us could have a sit-down, and I could tell them both about Vera-Mae's visit. I could also snag Wyatt's attention, and we could get over to Mac's ... for that search that was supposed to happen yesterday ... and maybe find Miranda's diary.

As soon as BJ went past and out the front door of the building, I went into Wyatt's office. He looked up and his lips went wide.

Oh, what that man can do just showing his teeth.

The response was automatic; I smiled back. He looked so happy to see me.

"Maggie," he said in greeting. "You're looking...," he frowned, "... stressed."

Chapter Seven

I FROWNED, TOO. "Stressed?"

He swallowed. "Everything okay? This case getting to you, too?"

I opened my mouth, then closed it. He could diffuse my irritations so easily ... too easily, sometimes. What is it about a man who expresses concern for a woman, even as he realizes he's committed a *faux pas?*

"Um. Yeah, I guess. I had a couple of ... interesting visitors while you were gone."

"I'm sorry, Maggie."

I waved off the apology. "Unless you're the killer, you don't have anything to be sorry for."

He stood and came around the desk. "Come on. I'll take you to lunch, and you can tell me all about your stressful morning." He took my arm and pulled me along, grabbing his hat on the way through.

Skidding past my workstation, I managed to snag my notes and my purse before stumbling out the door.

"Wanna take a walk?" Not waiting for an answer, he lengthened his stride down the sidewalk, still holding me by the arm. "Annetta's shouldn't be crowded at this hour."

"Sure. Yeah. Okay." Practically running, I hadn't started huffing yet, but I knew if he kept up the pace, I'd be breathless before we got there. At his height, he's got a lot of—good solid-muscled—leg.

I've always been on the tall side, topping out at five-eight in the eighth grade, but he and Ricky tower over me. Having to look down at most of the guys in my class, until my senior year, I vowed that excess height would play a major role in the choosing of my eventual mate. That's not the only attribute on my man-list, but it's in the top ten.

See, height does matter.

Inside Annetta's, we were surprised ... at least I was, at the crowd. We were lucky to get a back booth. Wyatt sat facing the front door with me facing him.

He scanned the menu for about half a second, and put it down. I studied mine like there would be a test later, and decided on turkey and cheddar, again.

Annetta herself came to take our order. She winked at Wyatt, and grinned at me—wiggling her eyebrows. I frowned and shook my head; she smirked and clicked her pen.

"What'll it be?"

"I'd like the ultimate burger platter and a Pepsi. Better bring a pitcher."

"Right." She nodded and jotted while snapping her gum. "Maggie?"

I opened my mouth, and in that instant, changed my mind. "I was going to order my usual, but, instead, I'll have a Philly steak and cheese, with peppers and onions. Fries on the side ... and a Pepsi." I paused. "On second thought, I'll just share his pitcher."

"Hey, that sounds pretty good. Can I change my order, Annetta?"

"Sure. Two Philly's comin' up." The pen disappeared in her hair, and she to the kitchen.

"Man, I haven't been here for a sit-down meal since … since Dodge Peters's wife clubbed him over the head for getting drunk on their twentieth wedding anniversary. How long's that been?" Wyatt leaned back in his seat, laughing. "'Bout a year, I guess. I couldn't believe how pissed off she was. Poor guy. I dragged him in here for coffee. Ended up ordering a whole meal." He shook his head. "I gotta admit, the smells … aroma, makes my mouth water every time."

"Yeah, I know what you mean. Betsy forgave him, especially after getting that new bedroom suite she'd been after him to buy."

"Yeah, but not for about three weeks … until the Classic Furniture store delivered it up from Morgantown."

"That was something to see, Dodge Peters, all humble and meek."

"She never lets him forget it, either."

"As is her right."

"They've got a special relationship, though. I envy them."

"Yeah. It's great." I frowned, distracted. "Now, that's odd." I commented, watching Annetta taking orders from the tables. "She's usually behind the counter."

"Does seem a bit shorthanded."

"Mmm hmm," I looked around for Annetta's help. "I know Susie works evenings. Maybe I've just never come in for lunch. I've done hoagie-runs, but can't remember staying to eat."

"Me, neither. Well, not for a long while, anyway. Shame, too. The food's great. I'll have to start coming in more often, for a 'dining-in' experience. What d'ya think?"

"I'm sure Annetta will appreciate it. With the fan club that's *bound* to follow you in, she'll make a killing. She may even have to start giving you kickbacks."

"Shut up." He laughed.

"Hey." Annetta set the tray down and playfully smacked Wyatt's arm with the back of her hand. "That's no way to talk to a lady." She unloaded the pitcher of soda and set a full glass in front of each of us.

"I was just telling him that if he came in more often, your business would pick up because of all the fans that'd follow him in. Then you'd have to pay him for advertising."

"Shut up." Annetta snickered. "Your orders will be out shortly. Anything I can get you 'til it's ready?"

I shook my head.

Wyatt ran a hand through his hair. "'Bout time to get to the barber."

"No it's not," Annetta and I both respond.

I glare at the woman as Wyatt answers: "Thanks, Annetta, maybe I'll hold off a bit ... and no," Wyatt glances towards my no- smiling face, "I think we're fine."

"Okay, then. Be good." She left to greet another few customers.

Leaning on his elbows, Wyatt stared.

The intensity of the look had me mentally scrambling. This was a business lunch, right? We were here to talk about business. Yes. Yes we were.

But, that look....

"So, Magdalena."

Darn it all, anyway. I love it when he uses my full name—well, not the whole thing. Really, it would take forever to get that all out. But, when he calls me *Magdalena*, his voice gets all deep and low and sultry-sounding.

Shivers me timbers.

"Who stressed you out?"

I had to wait to answer his question because Annetta arrived with our orders. She set down the plates and took a catsup bottle from her apron pocket. "Need anything else?"

We shook our heads. She nodded and left.

His question had sounded almost patronizing; I hoped he was sincere.

"First, Vera-Mae Wellington stopped in."

"Really? What'd she want?"

"To talk to you. Was going to come in a couple days ago, but got waylaid. Monday, she was so anxious to get to town, she hurried a little too much. Banged up her leg falling down the stairs."

"Miz Wellington?" He straightened. "Didn't break anything, did she? Why'd she need to see me? What was so important she came all the way to town on a bad leg? What'd the doctors say? Where's Bernice? She usually drives her around."

I held up a hand and echoed a phrase the woman had used on me. "One thing at a time." I then, between bites of juicy steak and cheese, proceeded to tell him her tale.

"I can see how you'd be concerned, but that doesn't sound like much of a stressor." He took a big bite of sandwich and half the peppers and onions fell on his plate. He made a face and used his fork to stuff them back in.

I tried not to laugh; mine was soon going to do the same thing. "No, you're right, but she imparted a lot of interesting information. A few minutes after she left, though, Forsythia Morgan dropped in, wanting to know all about Miz Wellington's visit." I told him everything that busybody had said. "After *she* left, BJ came in. But he didn't add any ... *stress*."

Wyatt rolled his eyes. "Now it makes more sense. Forsythia's hard to take even when she meets you on the street. Can never get rid of 'er."

"Oh, I got rid of her; no words passed these lips. Let's just say her irritated feathers were stuck up every which way."

He gave a short laugh. "Good. I suppose it's too much to hope for that she won't be back. Just wish she hadn't upset you so much."

"Glad you finally see my point. Except, I didn't realize I looked so bad. Maybe I should start wearing makeup." Boy, was that backhanded, or what? He'd either retreat and regroup with an apology, or flat out tell me he thought I looked good enough without all the goop.

"Now, Maggie, I didn't mean you didn't look good. Just, a bit frazzled."

"Frazzled!" That was even worse than stressed.

CHAPTER EIGHT

"NOT IN A bad way," he backpedaled. "I mean …
you know … you looked like you could use a change
of scenery. I know this case is driving *me* nuts. I can't
sleep. And Mac's been calling and crying on my
shoulder, sometimes literally."

My annoyance evaporated as he continued.

"Driving out to the lake … telling the man his
daughter's been murdered was about the hardest thing
I've ever had to do. Now, I have to go invade his
house to look for some small piece of evidence. To
search her room for something she might have left
behind, something the county cops missed, or didn't
bother looking for. And then, *then*, I have to tell him
the new developments from the past two days."

"You haven't done it yet? I thought you were
going to do that yesterday?"

"I was, but…." He let out a long breath. "I, he
was such a mess. I didn't get to it."

"Wyatt—"

He held up a hand. "I know. I know."

"Your job's harder than mine, even Ricky's, but
you know we're here for you." I reached across the
table and laid my fingers on his. "I'm speaking for
Ricky, but he'd agree. If you need anything … to talk,
cry, vent, anything at all … call me. I don't care what
time; day or night."

His hand clasped mine, gave it a squeeze.

"Thanks, Maggie. Appreciate it. Goes both ways, okay?"

"Yes. I'll remember."

"So, did anything else happen?"

"Nothing. Having a hard time getting my head around this whole thing, that's all. Does Mac know we're coming over today?"

He nodded. "Not a specific time, but, he knows. He got agitated when I told him I needed to look around, especially since the state and county's already been through. He said whenever, but I'll still give him a buzz when we get back and firm up a time. Two okay for you?"

"Is that when you're going to tell him about—" I paused, glancing around to see if anyone was listening in, then leaned across the table and whispered, "… the baby?"

"I plan to. I doubt he'll be in any better shape than he was the past few days, but I *have* to tell him. The longer I wait, the worse it'll be."

I nodded. "Are you going out to talk to Miz Wellington? She's gonna make up a special batch of mint juleps, just for your visit."

I smiled over my Pepsi.

Wyatt chuckled. "I just bet she will. Sounds like she gave you a pretty detailed account. Would you type up those notes for me? Probably won't get out there 'til tomorrow, but I'll need to take a copy with me, for reference."

"Done. Just needs to be printed."

"Glad you were the one hired."

"What does that—"

"You're always just so on-it, getting stuff done

and TCB'ing without having to be asked."

Grinning wide, I was about to say think-nothing-of it when Annetta came back to the table. "Well, kids, looks like lunch agreed with you." She collected the plates. "You up for dessert?"

"Ugh, no, I'm stuffed." I rummaged for my wallet.

Wyatt dug for his, too. "I got it. Annetta, the check?"

I compromised. "Okay, fine. I'll get the tip."

"Okay." He nodded. "I'll let ya."

Annetta had her hands on her hips. "You two on a date, or is the town picking up the tab?"

"Neither," we both answered, eyes locking.

"Uh huh." She handed Wyatt the ticket. "Just leave it on the table, if you want. I gotta go check on a coupla orders."

I found a five, and almost pouted; it was the only cash in my purse. But, since I'd opened my big mouth and stuck my foot in, I'd now have to chew around the toes.

Wyatt slid out and left exact change under the check. Reluctantly, my bill went on top, and we left.

Back at the office, the printer was spitting out pages when Ricky came in. I looked up as he took off his hat.

"Hey."

"Hey, Maggie." He wiped the sweat from his

brow. "Hoo-wee, sure is getting hot out there."

Surprise, surprise. "Really? Hadn't noticed."

"Yeah, I know. You get so used to the air-conditioning, you don't realize what the outside temperature is, 'til you leave."

Well, that wasn't what I meant, but I wasn't about to enlighten him. Wyatt and I had walked all the way to Annetta's and back, and I hadn't even noticed the heat.

He headed for Wyatt's office as the printer stopped. "Ricky, could you grab that when you go in to see Wyatt? And, please, ask him what time he wants to leave for Mac's."

"Roger."

After their briefing, of which I was not included, they both came out of Wyatt's office. Ricky went to his desk. Wyatt came over to mine.

"Mac's home. He said whenever's fine."

I nodded and rubbed my temples. It'd been my suggestion to search for a diary. Now that it was time, my feet were stuck to the floor. There was only one reason why. I didn't want to see the grief in Mac's face or hear it in his voice. When my husband died, dealing with the pain, the grief, had been monstrously hard. Understanding that, and knowing someone else was living it, was going to be a test of strength.

There was another, underlying, reason. One I was loathe to take out and look at; actually it was something I had to force into a dark closet in my brain. As long as I kept it under wraps, I would be able to deal. Helping Mac through this traumatic time, even if it was just his knowing there was support available, would ease the growing tightness in my chest. Maybe. "Okay." Still didn't want to go.

"I told you the state and county boys already went through the house, her bedroom, mainly looking for a suicide note. They didn't find one—didn't think they would—or anything else of significance."

I looked at him. "I'm really nervous. You're sure you want me to go along?"

Hands went to his hips, and he chuffed. "You're the one who wanted to go. It was your idea in the first place. Besides, I feel guilty enough by myself. I need the support."

"Why do you feel guilty?"

"I'm the one who gave him the news. He's a good friend. Miranda was my goddaughter, for Pete's sake." He leaned against my desk and crossed his arms. "I can't let out my grief while I'm around him because *I'm* supposed to be the professional. *I'm* the one in charge. I'm supposed to *find* her killer. And I haven't even told him the worst part, yet."

"What part?" Then it dawned on me. "Oh, Wyatt. You haven't told him it wasn't suicide? I thought … you said at lunch you hadn't told him about the baby, but I thought you at least had told him it wasn't a suicide."

"I'm a coward, okay? If I get a chance to talk to him alone while we're there, I'll say something. If not, I'll do it … *tonight*. I have to go over there anyway, for moral support, or mutual commiseration, whatever. Just, don't be surprised by anything weird that happens tomorrow. I may have a huge hangover. And if I'm late coming in, pretend I've been out taking statements, or something."

I picked up my purse. "Procrastination."

"Absolutely. Investigating a crime, I can handle that. Being personally involved—being friends with—the victim's family? No way. I find I'm questioning my patterns, my abilities, my instincts. Will I bring in the right person? Will I find the right clues to solve the crime?

"I have to tell my friend, 'Hey, I have good news. Your daughter didn't commit suicide. Bad news, one of the upstanding citizens of Mossy Creek did it. Then, worse, she was carrying the only grandchild you're never going to get.'

"So, yeah, I procrastinate when I have to go over to Mac's."

"I'm sorry, Wyatt," I said, quietly. "But, you shouldn't question yourself. You're a great cop. If we, as a town, didn't think you were able to do your job, the council wouldn't have hired you."

"Amen to that," Ricky crowed.

"And," I began, to lighten the heavy mood, "if you couldn't do your job, your fan club would disown you."

Fast, Wyatt snatched his hat and swung it. Quick on my feet, I sashayed my hip. A miss! Yeah, I'm good. And was out the door heading for the Suburban provided by the council for the Chief's use—Wyatt in pursuit—before he could try again.

I could hear Ricky laughing from his corner.

"You keep talking about this fan club of mine," Wyatt opened the passenger door for me. "How come I've never seen any of 'em? Can you name even one?"

He shut the door and went around to his own side. The man had the manners of a true gentleman. He hadn't even thought about what he was doing, it was that automatic. In awe, I waited until he got in and buckled his seatbelt.

"Thank you, Wyatt."

He grabbed me with his eyes, his hand on the ignition. "Maggie, you have to answer one question, before you make me ask another."

"Oh. Sorry. What was the question? I got distracted."

"See, there you go again." He shook his head and started the diesel. "The question was: Where is this fan club? I've never seen it." He put the big SUV in gear and pulled onto the road.

"You *really* have no idea, do you?"

"If I did, I wouldn't have asked."

"Surely you know that anywhere you go, you're watched."

He gave me a quick confused glance. "Never really thought about it."

"UN-BELIEV-ABLE," I muttered. "Wyatt, you are … um … for wont of a better word—a hunk. You're tall, well-built, and you fill out a uniform, very-very nicely. You're in a position of authority. And the *pièce de résistance*, the absolutely best part? You're blessedly single. Every woman in this town, old or young, single or married, *droools* over you. Shoot, Miz Wellington thinks you're … oh, how did she put it? … quite dishy."

I spread out my hands. "And, the men? The men in this town envy you to the point of hero worship. They want to be like you. Hell, they want to *be* you."

"Stop, Maggie, please! You're giving me a complex. That stuff is just *not* true. It can't be. I'd have noticed."

I wasn't done. "Who do the girls call when they need help? Ricky?" I shook my head. "He wishes, but, sadly, no. They call for Wyatt. When Forsythia came by to spy on Vera-Mae, did she ask to see Ricky? No. Did she actually want to talk to me? Certainly not. She asked for you. When you go past the bakery, and you look in the window, who do you see? A cream-filled donut, that's what. Do you know what Vicki's thinking about as she's biting her lip and moaning?"

"Come on, Maggie. What does all that have to do with a fan club?"

"Wyatt, the whole town's a fan. People follow you wherever you go, just to be where you are."

Silence for two whole blocks. At the stop sign on Poplar Street, he looked over at me. "Really?"

I slowly nod. "Really."

"How about you, Maggie? Are *you* a fan?"

I smiled, or grimaced, depending on your point of view; now, bite-your-fingernails nervous. "I'm at the top of the list."

His face changed expression, but I can't explain how. "What … you drool over me?"

Uh oh. Too close for comfort. I drew in a breath and said, "Um, yeah. I do."

"All those things you listed a minute ago, that's what you think about me?"

I glance down. "Wyatt, that's what I know. And I'm not the only one."

I wished I was.

He turned his attention back to driving, and we went around the corner. "Hmm."

I bit my lip.
Good God, what did I just do?

CHAPTER NINE

WE PULLED UP in front of Mac's brick ranch. I don't know how he did it, but Wyatt was out of the vehicle and around to my door before I even got my seatbelt off. His lack of reaction to my honesty was still bothering me, but when I looked at him, he was smiling.

That lasted until we got to the front door, then he was all business.

He knocked.

We had to wait a minute, until a haggard-looking MacLean Richards opened the door and gestured us inside.

I didn't think about what I was doing, instinct had me walking over to the poor man. My arms wrapped around him, my head on his chest. He started blubbering and held tight. I sobbed with him. This was the first time I'd let my guard down and shown my grief for Miranda. It was too hard to deal with on a personal level, for a couple of big reasons. Though my sons are grown, I'm still a mom.

We stood like that, Mac and me, for several minutes, 'til Mac's weeping subsided.

"Thanks, Maggie." He nodded and wiped his eyes on his shirtsleeve. "Go wherever you need to. Her room's second on the right, at the top of the stairs."

Before my eyes, Wyatt and Mac's handshake transformed into the kind of hug that no one ever wants to see. I dug in my purse for a tissue and blew my nose.

"Please, just find out what happened to my little girl."

I looked at Wyatt. He shook his head and motioned me towards the stairs. Not happy with him, I went up.

As Wyatt checked out the ground floor, I concentrated on Miranda's bedroom. There didn't seem much point in going through the whole house again, since who knows how many law enforcement officers had already rifled through everything, finding zilch.

Then again, they'd only been looking for a suicide note, and had probably done a search for drugs, and other paraphernalia associated with suspicious deaths. We were on a more focused mission; we knew the victim, might see something they missed.

Miranda was ... *had* been, a tidy housekeeper, at least when it came to her room. Her nightstand drawers held miscellaneous pens and scraps of notebook paper with odd nonsense quotes, small photo albums of various events she'd attended, an unopened box of condoms, and a battered address book, but no letters ... and no diary.

Going through a teen's dresser was something I had always made a point of *not* doing. It was creepy, for one, and felt like an invasion of privacy. The state of affairs, in too many households these days, makes it almost a necessity, but not for me.

I told my boys to keep their things straightened, including their dresser drawers. They did, for the most part. I'd put their laundry—all neatly folded—

—

71

on their beds. Their job was to put it away.

Miranda's things were nicely in place, and it didn't take long to see that there wasn't a diary amongst her delicates, or under her jeans. It was possible she hadn't kept one; some girls don't, but I wasn't finished, yet.

I could tell her room had been gone through, probably the county boys. There was an empty space on her desk, presumably where her computer had been.

Nothing exciting in any of the three drawers.

The closet was about as full as it could get without being over-crowded. Dresses, shirts, pants, and skirts, all hung up on scented, or otherwise frilly girlish hangars. Even her bathrobe and jammies were hanging from a hook on the backside of the door. The floor was jumbled with shoes—though all were paired—with boxes of more stacked along the back wall. The upper shelf was crammed with sweatshirts, sweaters, old yearbooks, and: Oh, cool. LP's! I didn't think anybody under thirty had long-playing vinyl record albums anymore, or even knew what they were.

Back in the corner on a hook was a denim jacket, pockets bulging more than normal. The left held a wad of tissues—thankfully unused—and some fuzz-covered mints. In the right, I found a couple paper clips, a crumbled piece of lime-green notepaper, a gum wrapper, and … HOLY COW! A man's class ring: a big gold chunky thing with a dark red gem set in the center.

The light in the closet left a lot to be desired, and I couldn't read the lettering. I'd have to wait until we got back to the office so I could use my magnifying glass. I was so excited I almost dropped the clunky thing, before tucking it—and the piece of paper—into my back pocket.

"You about ready?"

I looked over my shoulder and saw Wyatt in the hallway. "I'd like to go through these boxes."

He shrugged and leaned against the wall. "Go ahead, but I doubt there's anything more than shoes. Especially since county already blew through this place. If they found anything of significance, they took it with them. But, it's up to you."

I tapped a tooth with a fingernail while studying the inside of the cramped closet. "You're right. It's probably pointless." There was one, *obvious* place I hadn't checked, yet. And, I'm not above asking for muscle when necessary. "Help me lift the mattress?"

"It's not that heavy, is it?"

He came into the room.

I gave him a look. "No, Einstein, but I don't want it to slide off. Why make more of a mess than we need to?"

He shrugged and bent to grasp one of the corners. "You think she hid it under here?" He grunted as he hefted the Queen-sized Serta. And there it was, a traditional little pink book, complete with keyed-clasp.

"Most girls I knew growing up kept their diaries under their mattress, or in their nightstand drawer, but this is a pretty obvious hiding place. My question, why bother hiding it at all?"

I picked up the small journal, and Wyatt let go of the bedding.

"Now, how do we get it open?"

"It'd be easy enough to break, but...." I stopped Wyatt with a finger as I went to the jewelry box on the dresser. "Girls, ninety-nine percent of the time, keep their keys in these." I breathed a sigh of relief when I saw the tiny gold key nested in red velvet. Turning, beaming, I held it aloft.

Wyatt clapped. "Figures you'd be right again. And that's good; at least we've found something. Sure wasn't anything downstairs. Least nothing that would give us a clue as to who killed her." He lifted the gold pendant that hung from a gold chain around my neck—my version of a watch. I had to hold my breath. "Getting late ... what do you say, super snoop, ready to go? Oh, and just for your information, I told Mac it wasn't suicide." We exchanged a knowing look. "I'll tell him the rest tonight over a bottle of Jimmy B."

"I can understand that. Even though it doesn't bring her back, knowing she didn't take her own life is.... It's just better." Mollified, mostly, I dropped the little book and its key into my purse. "Okay, then. Let's go."

With Wyatt heading out of the room, and I followed him down the stairs.

Mac stood by the newel post. "Find anything?"

"What we did should help a lot. Thanks for letting us come by."

He nodded; teared up again. "Anything to help. I just don't understand...."

"That's okay." Biting my cheek, I glanced at Wyatt, still annoyed with him keeping so much from his friend. Then again, he knew the man, indeed, had shared a pact with him. I let the moment stand for some heartbeats, then took Mac's hand in my own. "Stay in touch, Mac. If you need *anything*, call me. Okay?" I gave him a farewell hug.

Feeling the man's wiry arms rise and squeezing in kind, told me he knew he could.

Wyatt's words broke the embrace. "Again, I'll be back … later tonight," he reminded.

Mac's mouth threatened to grin. "We're *Binging-it* tonight, right? And you're in charge of the ammo."

"Just like I promised."

"But don't get crazy with the Foghorns; m'mood's more set on the other."

Wyatt chuckled. "No problem, I'm already there with ya."

This time no cheek-biting would prevent any mirthful approval. Binging has been popular in local parts since my dad's prime. Jim Beam and buffalo wings (the more lava the better), though some understandably preferred Jack Daniels, Jameson, or others. The combination fit for men during times of loss, local games, Super Bowls, or just simple Friday night get-togethers: cronies and buddies alike, all backslapping, cards, and cigars.

Mac and Wyatt sharing a Bing night would be a chance for them to deepen their bond, pouring out their mutual grief, but in a safe way … where their egos could save face, even as they enjoyed one another's company and the opportunity to vent their sorrow.

Mac waved us off the porch and we got into the SUV, depression, excitement, terror, all sorts of things hanging over our heads. Why? There was

Miranda, of course, ever present, but then there'd my admission, and the Gordian knot it had left in my stomach, and of what would be happening next.

Back at the station, and at my desk, I slung my purse down-and-under, pulled out my chair and— *OUCH*. Something sharp had stabbed my right hipbone. Frowning and massaging the offended area, I felt the hard lump of the treasure I'd found. Holy Hannah. "WYATT!"

I dug it out of my pocket as he came barreling out of the office.

"What? What's wrong?"Ricky scrambled, too, hurrying to help. "What's wrong, Maggie?"

"I forgot about it, believe that? Once we found the diary, I just—Wyatt, look." I held out the ring. "This was in the pocket of her jean-jacket. There was a piece of paper crumbled up in it, too." My other hand went for it, and Wyatt grabbed the ring.

Ricky looked on, grinning. "Where's it from?"

Wyatt squinted at the small lettering on the side. "A college, I think. Here, Rick. See if you can make it out. It's pretty worn down."

The boy studied it, took it over to his desk and turned on the lamp to get a better look. Even borrowed my magnifying glass, to no avail. "Nah." He shook his head and brought the ring back. "It's about wore off. Could take it over to Tate's Jeweler's."

"Good idea." Wyatt motioned for him to keep it. "And for God's sake, don't lose it?"

I un-wadded the small square of green and turned it right-side up. "Well, shoot."

"Now what?"

"Says: 'Meet me on Foggy Bottom Road at 10. Can't wait, sweets. LB.' Who's LB?"

"LB?" Ricky scratched his head. "I can't think of anybody with those initials."

"Me, either."

Wyatt snapped his fingers. "A nickname, maybe … or, something she called him?"

"Wait a minute." Ricky caught hold of my arm. "There's a cheerleader named Leticia Bradley … Lettie. I questioned her."

"She wouldn't call Miranda *sweeets*."

He shrugged. "My mom used to call my sister sweets every once in a while."

"Or," I proposed. "Maybe Miranda intercepted it."

"Or," Wyatt added. "Maybe she was supposed to deliver it."

I nodded. "Hmm. Yeah, could be. But it was all crumpled up."

"So?"

"Well, usually, if I have a note I'm done with, I crumble it."

"Maybe she was jealous of Lettie," Ricky reasoned. "She could have found the note, crumbled it, and kept it so whoever was supposed to get it, wouldn't. Hell, maybe Lettie's gay."

"Or maybe Miranda delivered it, and whoever it was intended for read it, crumbled it, gave it back to her, and she never threw it out."

"Enough." Wyatt massaged his temples for a moment, then resumed. "Let's not get too carried away. The note may or may not be relevant to the crime, but it is significant of something." He ran his hands over his face. "Maggie, from now on you're in charge of all the material evidence we collect—save the ring, least 'til Ricky brings it back."

"Hey, we finally get to use that locker in the back."

Wyatt chuckled. "Forgot the damn thing was there." Wyatt's faced turned serious. "Log everything we have so far. I'll get you the key. It doesn't leave your sight."

"Wyatt, I've been doing this job a long time." I'd thrown off his momentum.

"Of course you have, I'm sorry." A pause. "Rick, take that ring over to Tate's. See if Tilly or Mike can tell us anything."

"Roger, boss." Pocketing the ring, Ricky spun, grabbed his hat, and went out.

Wyatt stood.

And smiled.

Mmm.

"Great work, Magdalena."

Oh, crap! One of these days, he was going to melt me into a puddle doing that.

"Thank you, Wyatt." My lashes almost fluttered.

"Now. You need to keep a log—"

"I know. You said that already." I frowned. "I *have* been keeping a log."

"Excellent." He winked and returned to his office.

Irritated, hands on my hips, I watched him. Apparently, he wasn't going to apologize for insulting my intelligence.

My body, though, was absorbing all the glow and warmth and … WOW energy, from the last fifteen minutes. My body won. I had to sit down, or my knees would've buckled.

But my brain was still not happy.

I decided to take the diary home to read. Wyatt insisted it should be me—since I was female. Sounded sexist, but I didn't protest. Why should it matter who read it? Miranda wouldn't be objecting. It did make me feel like a snoop, and if circumstances had been different, I wouldn't have been anywhere near it.

I did read it over, and have to admit, it was shocking. I've never read anything more boring in all my life. Well, maybe not the *most* boring. I remember back in high school…. But, that's a different story. Suffice it to say, it was the mother of all yawners. How had she stayed so popular?

No secret rendezvous, no 'so and so got caught smoking in the girls' bathroom,' no 'Missy Sue got caught kissing … *anybody* … behind the bleachers.' No juice. All she'd written down were dates, appointments, and sporting events—nothing but a bunch of pocket lint.

Humdrum.

Where were all the intimate thoughts and racy shenanigans of an active teenage cheerleader? And if it was just a calendar, why lock it? Why bother to hide it? Who would care when she had a hair appointment, or had to babysit?

I pondered. Could this drivel be a decoy? If so,

why the need for two? DUH! The other one's too hot for prying eyes. But, whose eyes was she trying to keep out? And, what was so secret?

Wyatt and Ricky were going to be disappointed when I told them the only things I found, even remotely interesting, were the little hearts she drew around the nights she was babysitting.

Now, that could have been because she really liked babysitting little Kendall, or, because she was meeting her boyfriend afterward.

I wondered if Ricky's sister had kept a diary when she was in high school. Maybe she could tell us—in generalities, at least—what she wrote in hers. I never kept a *Little Miss Secret*, not for more than two weeks at a time, if that long.

I fell asleep and dreamt of dates and hearts ... and Wyatt.

CHAPTER TEN
THURSDAY....

THE MAN WAS already in his office and on the phone when I got there. Boy, what a shocker that was. Can't remember a time when he got to work before me. He'd warned us about maybe having a hangover, but never even a whisper about possibly beating me here. Maybe this was the 'something weird' he'd mentioned in the same conversation.

What else would get him here this early? Better not be another death.

Not wanting to interrupt his call—although I really wanted to know whom he was talking to, and why—I bided my time. He'd tell me when he was ready, but I'm so curious by nature—Mama calls it nosey. It irked me royal, not being close enough to hear the conversation.

I set the donuts from Corsair's Market on the table, and proceeded to make coffee, just like always, trying my hardest to overhear … something. His door was open, but he was talking kind of low—not that he was trying to keep me from hearing on purpose.

Then, just as his voice raised enough for me to hear actual words, the front door crashed opened. I turned around and gasped, nearly dropping the coffee grounds. "Wylie-James!"

He took a few steps into the room, and crumpled to the floor.

I threw the grounds in the trash and hurried over. "CHIEF."

I knelt beside Wylie-James. *Holy Limburger Cheese, Batman.* The man stunk. I made a face as my stomach pretzled. It was hard to tell whether the odor was actually coming from him or his clothing. Not that it mattered; both were in bad shape.

His shirt and pants were torn and caked with mud, or *eeuww*, worse. A large bruise started midway on his forehead, just above the left eyebrow and purpling all the way to an ear. Crown to heel, scratches and abrasions, small cuts and ill-formed scabs adorned what skin I could see, let-alone his face.

Wyatt hurried out of his office, and pushed me aside.

Happy to be away from the stench, I called for an ambulance.

"Maggie, what happened?"

Like I was supposed to know.

Phone to an ear, I shrugged. "He just walked in— well, stumbled more like—then collapsed, right where you see him."

"He alive?"

I rolled my eyes. "You didn't give me a chance to find out. He seems to be breathing."

He laid two fingers to Wylie's jugular while I waited for the hospital dispatcher to answer.

"*Yess.*" There was relief in his voice. "His heart's beating pretty strong." He grimaced. "What's that smell?"

"It ain't me. He's the one been swimming in a pigsty."

He wrinkled his nose. "Smells like it, too."

I held up a hand for silence, and requested the ambulance. "Curiouser and curiouser." Quick peek over Wyatt's shoulder. "Wonder where he's been all this time."

"Hopefully he'll come around pretty quick and tell us." Wyatt got to his feet.

I wondered, too. *Hmm*. Maybe Wylie-James's' disappearance was connected to the murder. Why come here, instead of going to the hospital? That would have been more logical, given that he passed out as soon as he got in the door. Breathing through my mouth, I stared at the comatose man.

In mere minutes, I could hear the siren. The front door burst open—second time this morning—and Ricky blew in.

"What's going on?" He stopped and looked around, almost in a panic. "I heard the call for an ambulance on the scanner." Taking a moment to calm down, he focused on me.

I pointed to the prone body.

"Who's that?" He moved closer.

"Wylie-James."

He wrinkled his nose. "What's that smell?"

"Wylie-James."

"Man, he been rolling around in a cow pasture?"

Nodding, I stuck to my original assessment. "Pigsty." Stubbornness runs in my family … both sides.

He nodded back. "That, too."

So much nicer when they agree.

Snagging his sleeve, I pulled him closer to my desk. "You might want to step over here … gonna need some room for the stretcher."

Two burly paramedics wheeled a gurney through our battered door. It was a bit of a squeeze, but they managed. Didn't take them long to get Wylie-James strapped on; he's only skin and bone.

They took his vitals and hooked up an IV before transporting him to the hospital. Wyatt told them to please have him contacted when Wylie-James came to, and that he or Ricky would be by shortly for a report. They said they'd pass along the request to the ER.

By the time the fuss was over, the coffee pot had finished dripping, and I needed a mug like a boozer needs their sauce. I decided the morning warranted a donut, too. Sweets are a big temptation for me, but most days I can resist. Either that or buy bigger clothes.

That's not gonna happen.

I was still dying to know who'd been on the phone with Wyatt so early this morning. Thought I'd forgotten about that, huh? I may be the dispatcher and administrative specialist extraordinaire, and whatever else they need, but I know better than to stick m'nose into the police chief's business ... except, of course, when he decides to include me. So far today, he had not.

I sniffed—indignantly.

Stingy man.

Yeah, I know, with all the excitement, he hadn't even had time for a mug of joe, and it was only nine o'clock.

Ricky paced in front of the box of Corsair's: éclairs, cream-filleds, and long johns. Nervous, he'd snagged three already—his normal quota. So, when he reached for another, I cleared my throat. He stopped his zigzagging and looked over.

"Chief hasn't had any, yet."

He sighed, and skulked to his corner desk. "Maggie?"

I watched him over the lip of my steaming java. "Yes, Ricky?"

"S'pose Wylie-James knows anything about Randy's death?"

I smiled. "Great minds think alike."

"Huh?"

"I've been wondering the same thing."

"Oh, yeah? Hah. I guess we'll have to wait 'til he wakes up to find out."

"Umm, yes. I would think so."

"Well, shoot. I know we can't ask him anything; the man's unconscious." He stopped and tilted his head. "Well, we *could* ask; he just wouldn't answer."

I rolled my eyes, but didn't say a word. Yeah, sometimes he acts the hick.

Wyatt came out of his office far enough to say in a controlled whisper, "I need to talk to both of you." He put a hand to the side of his head. "And bring me a donut and some coffee … and make it a double."

CHAPTER ELEVEN

RICKY AND I looked at each other and got up to join our boss. Ricky handled the coffee and donuts— took the whole box of two with him. I backtracked and grabbed my notepad and pen. Just in case.

Neither Rick, nor I, snickered. But, we wanted to.

Wyatt sat at his desk writing on a legal pad. Ricky set the box of donuts on the corner of the desk, and the cup of coffee right in front of Wyatt, who stopped writing. The man took a big sip. With a sound of satisfaction, he leaned back in his chair. "I realize there is some curiosity about why I was here so early."

Why was he looking at me?

"Mac and I were up most of the night, and by the time we were done, I'd forgotten how to drive. Once the rooster crowed, I figured it better to just come straight in."

I smiled.

He continued, looking amused. "I was on the phone with Mac, before Wylie-James showed up."

Aha!

"Says his daughter's is car missing. Now y'all know, he was out on the lake when this all happened. When he got back, he saw her car was gone. Didn't dawn on him until this morning that it was actually gone. If it wasn't in the garage, then where was it? Not at the crime scene, that's for sure."

Sitting straight up, he smacked himself in the

forehead—*lightly*. Ricky and I exchanged looks with questioning eyes. Wyatt shook his head. "No. Listen. If she committed suicide, her car would have been out at the swimming hole!"

"Yeah, you're right. Man, are we thick or what? She couldn't have gotten out there unless she drove herself, somebody dropped her off, or she walked. I think we can eliminate one and three, don't you?"

Ricky was getting into the swing of it.

"So what happened to her car?" I dimmed the enthusiasm. "If it's not out at the swimming hole, and it's not at her dad's, and no one—so far as we know—reported seeing it anywhere, then where … is … it?"

Wyatt nodded. "Good question."

"We should have figured that out before now. I mean, Miz Wellington said someone carried her, or someone in a cheerleading outfit, towards the swimming hole, but came back empty-handed before taking off. Right there," I clapped my hands, "proof that she wasn't driving her own car!"

Ricky cleared his throat.

Wyatt stared.

"Someone killed her for her car?" Ricky shook his head. "Never mind. That's pretty idiotic."

Wyatt interrupted. "More like farfetched. The car was a clunker. And, maybe she wasn't driving it that night. Whatever the case, it's still missing."

I leaned forward. "Even so, now that we have more telling evidence, we need to figure out whether it's someone she knew, or a stranger? Or if her death was simply poor planning by the killer?"

Ricky frowned. "Poor planning?"

"Yeah." I nodded, and was about to continue with my theory when Wyatt butted in ... again.

"If the killer wanted her death to look like a suicide, he should have left her car for us to find, to *really* throw us off track. I'm not sure I'd call it poor planning, but I don't think it was supposed to happen. Could've been panic. Whoever it was, freaked out because she was dead. He, or she, wasn't prepared for that, and after stringing her up, took off in the car."

"Exactly." I nodded again. "He didn't *plan* for her to die."

Wyatt grinned, briefly.

"More or less," I added ... sort of like sticking your tongue out at your best friend in grade school.

The man looked frustrated.

Ricky scratched his head. "So we're back to square one?"

"Maybe Wylie-James can shed some light on the subject." Both men stared. "I just have a feeling." A shrug. "I mean why, in his exhausted condition, come all the way to the police station, unless he had something really important to tell us? I mean, the man practically went right past the hospital on the way here."

"He say anything before keeling over?" Wyatt leaned back in his chair, linking his fingers behind his head.

"Nope. He walked in. I said 'Wylie-James,' real surprised-like—because I was—and *boom!* the man was down."

"Damn weird, ya ask me."

I agreed.

Meeting done, Ricky and I went back to our

desks.

Wyatt and Ricky were due back from lunch when the phone rang. "Mossy Creek Police Department."

"Maggie, Caroline from the hospital. Chief in?"

"Not at the moment. Need to leave a message?"

"Dr. Lassiter wants the chief to know Mr. Forster is awake and asking for 'im."

"Oh, that's great. Thank you. I'll be sure to let him know. He's been rather anxious about the man."

"Sure. Bye."

Click.

I hung up just as Ricky and Wyatt walked through the door. "Hey, guys." They came over. I guess my voice had excitement in it, or something.

"What's up, Maggie?" Ricky sat down on the corner of my desk.

I looked at Wyatt. "Wylie-James is awake and asking to see you."

"Great." Wyatt elbowed Ricky. "Come on. Let's hear what he's got say."

"On your six, Boss."

"I need my notepad. Meet you outside."

"Roger that." Ricky made for the door, shoving his hat on his head.

"Wyatt, take a Steno." I held it out.

Wyatt took it. "Thanks, Maggie. See you when we get back."

I winked. "I'm not going anywhere."

A long eye-to-eye pause. "Good." He put his hat on.

I bit my lip.

He grinned. "Later."

I waited until the door shut and closed my eyes—just-for-a-minute. He was doing it again. "Maggie." I shook my head, resigned. "You've got it bad, kid. *Real* bad."

An hour later, filing paperwork and hearing them come back, I finished up and went to find them. They were in Wyatt's office. "So, what did he have to say?"

"A lot, actually." Wyatt kicked back in his chair and yawned. "We know where Miranda's car is."

"Really?" I took a seat. "Where?"

"Old Bear Creek Swamp." Ricky wagged his head. "Sucked it right in."

"What?"

"Yep." Wyatt straightened. "Almost got Wylie-James, too."

I sat back. "Oh no. Spill it … from the beginning."

"It was like this: Said he was out and about Sunday night and saw a car run off the road and into the swamp. By the time he got down over the back to the car, the front end was already partially submerged. He waited to see if anyone would crawl out. When no one did, he waded in, thinking they might be unconscious. Tried the driver's side, but it was too dark to see.

"He banged on the window, but got no response. By now, the car was listing pretty deep to the right, the front passenger side sinking fast. He moved 'round to look in the windshield and slipped; mud sucked him partway under the car."

My breath caught. My heart pounded. Worried for Wylie-James.

Wyatt continued. "Caught hold of the tire and pulled himself upright again, staggering in the deep muck. Himself now the priority, he abandoned the rescue attempt, hoping the car was empty and he wasn't leaving someone to die. He knew if he didn't get out of there, the mire would do him in, just like the car, and with no means of escape. He struggled, mostly slipping and sliding across the mud, toward the embankment."

Wyatt's hands rubbed his face. "You know how steep that one side is? He couldn't get out the way he went in. Said he felt like he wasn't going to make it to shore, or get out of there alive."

Ricky piped in. "Poor guy. Every time he stopped to rest, he went deeper, so he tried not to sit too long. Took him a couple hours, at least, to get to the far bank."

Wyatt again. "Just as he managed to flop onto solid ground, someone clocked his dome and it was bye-bye.

"Coming to, he started walking to town to get some help. He didn't realize how badly he'd been hurt 'til he got here, the spots came up, and he was lights out."

"Was real confused waking up in the hospital. The staff was ready to tie him to the bed, because he was threatening to leave. Calmed down when they told him the chief of police was on his way to talk to 'im." Ricky crossed his leg over his knee and bounced a foot. "Man's one lucky hound."

"No wonder he passed out. I don't suppose he saw who walloped him."

Wyatt shook his head. "Didn't even know what day it was. When he found out it was Thursday, he had a fit. Lost three days."

"Got clunked pretty good. That's like … that'd be a major concussion. Think it was the killer?"

"Y'think? Whoever it was, cost him half-a-week."

"Wish we had a forensics team like CSI has to analyze the car. Bet we could find out who drove it last."

Wyatt laughed. "Yeah. Wouldn't that be great? Our entire year's budget for all that equipment, plus the techs."

"Well, we did find out a couple things. Wylie-James isn't missing anymore, and neither is Miranda's car. Someone didn't want anyone to find it, or not for a while, at least, which reaffirms our murder theory." I was thinking, writing, and speaking at the same time. Wow, multi-tasking. "You'll need to call Mac."

"Yeah. Dodge, too, and have him tow that car out of the mire. But we can't say the investigation is at a stand-still." Wyatt leaned his elbows on the desk and steepled his fingers. "It is moving forward, just not fast enough."

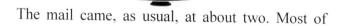

The mail came, as usual, at about two. Most of

our correspondence comes from other agencies. Some ask for information, some verify a request. Today, there were two marked PERSONAL for Wyatt. I never open those. When they come in, they're not for anyone else's eyes but his. I put 'em in his box.

He smiled at me.

Returning the look, I wished I could give him a sloppy wet one, but just turned around and walked out.

Half an hour later....

"Maggie?" Wyatt came out of his office, squinting at a sheet of paper in his hand.

"Yes?" I stopped typing and waited.

Halting a foot from my desk with a sheepish look on his face, he handed me the paper. "I forgot my glasses. Can you read this for me?"

Was he kidding? "Oh, come on, Wyatt. You don't wear glasses."

He didn't even crack a smile. "I don't wear them in public." He glanced around the room. "I didn't used to have to wear them here, but lately the print on these forms has been getting smaller and smaller."

Already wearing mine, I took the paper and shook it straight. "It says—" My eyes flew over the words. "Wyatt, this says—"

I looked at him.

He was grinning.

"Congratulations, Maggie!"

My jaw dropped, and I stared again at the official letterhead. A formal appointment from the borough, agreeing with Wyatt's recommendation, that I receive a peacekeeper's badge. No, I would not be authorized a firearm—*guess they don't trust me with one*—or wear a regulation uniform—*they'd be ugly*—but still and nonetheless WOULD be duly sworn in as a protector of the law and the residents of Mossy Creek.

The words began to blur. I realized tears were spilling, and blinked to clear my vision. "This is so *coool*. Thankyouthankyouthankyou. But, won't this…? I mean—"

Silence.

Wyatt stared, smiling. Then the smile vanished. Then his face stood concerned. And it had every right to. I was crestfallen. *Crud … what horrid timing.* The problem? Fraternization. Our relationship had just started to— And then there was our moment in the SUV where I had laid it all out—*gag, what was I thinking?* Now what? Was our budding relationship going to be stuck in the budding stage!

I tried to bring my smile back. "Does this mean we have to stop … uh, the flirting?" I figured that was a safe way to word it, since we hadn't actually made any real overt moves more involved than that.

Wyatt said something—under his breath.

"Did you just say—?"

"Not the word you think you heard." He crossed his arms. "I hadn't thought of that." He shrugged. "I mean, you can always refuse. And there's no pay raise, or anything attached. Really, it's just a token role. You can hold a suspect, but not arrest them. You can't carry a weapon. You'll still be assigned to the desk and dispatch, not to a car, or a routine cruising schedule, and—"

"Sounds like you're trying to talk me out of it." I could see the frustration on his face. "Wyatt, I'm really and truly honored. This means a lot to me," I held up the paper, "that you did this. I just.... I don't...."

I blew out a breath. "If it means I can't flirt, etcetera, with you, then maybe I shouldn't accept it. I don't want you to lose your job over it, and I definitely don't want to lose mine. But, I really like … um...."

There I was, at a loss for words.

Again.

He sat on the corner of my desk. "I'm sorry, Maggie. It seemed like a good thing when I did it. Ricky thought it'd be a hoot for you to have a badge, since you didn't have a private eye license. But, you're right, if it means we can't pursue a personal, uh, *friend-li-ness*, then I'll tell the council you turned it down."

"I don't want to make you feel bad for suggesting it, either."

"Don't worry, Maggie. This was a spur of the moment thing. You're not going to hurt my feelings. I know how much it means, both ways."

I smiled and almost patted his knee, until I remembered we didn't know each other well enough for that ... yet. "Thanks, Wyatt."

We sat enjoying each other's company for another few minutes, until the phone interrupted our mutual admiration moment. I put the caller on hold, so Wyatt could get to his desk.

He got up and strolled to his office, but turned at the last minute. "By the way, you were right, I don't wear glasses. And, for what it's worth, I'm glad you refused."

Wow. I had to fan myself … almost forgot to

transfer the call.

A few hours later, Ricky returned.

Even though I had decided Miranda's diary was bogus, I still hadn't talked to Wyatt or Ricky about my conclusions. At our—almost daily—afternoon briefing, I broached the subject.

They were disappointed. We were all envisioning hot torrid confessions. I, again, voiced my puzzlement about her need to conceal. Why would she have to hide something no one else was around to find ... or even look at? There had to be a reason for the deception.

The entries she'd made in the last week before she died *did* sound different ... more tense ... forced ... but, with no real emotion. I pointed out the fact that she also put little hearts around the days she babysat for the mayor's little son.

"My sister used to do something like that, whenever a boy she liked talked to her."

Silence in the room.

CHAPTER TWELVE

RICKY SPREAD HIS hands. "What?"

"You read your sister's diary?" Wyatt, fun-tugging at the corners of his mouth, studied his second in command.

Two pink spots daubed Ricky's cheeks. "When I was a bratty little brother, yeah. I needed to find out if she was snitching me out to mom and dad."

Wyatt scratched an arm. "About what?"

Ricky shifted in his seat and cleared his throat. "Kid stuff."

"Really?" My body screamed *spill it*. "I'm a mom; tell me what kind of kid stuff?" It was so much fun to tease him.

He swallowed nervously. "Look, it was a long time ago. I don't do stuff like that, anymore." He was starting to sweat.

"What stuff would that be?" I pressed without mercy. "The stuff your sister was snitching you out about? Or, that you were reading her diary?"

"Both. Look—"

"Stuff like what?" Wyatt, trying to hide a smirk, gave me a wink.

Ricky gave us a smug smile. "Stuff like reading my sister's diary." Then he laughed. "Had ya goin' there for a while, didn't I?"

"Why didn't you say so in the first place?" Wyatt let him off the hook, uncrossed his arms and looked back at me. "So, what's up with Randy's hearts?"

"I'll have to think about it some more, but it could be she was falling for the mayor's kid … he is a real cutie. There's more to this, though."

"You don't think they're connected to the little guy?"

I shook my head. "No, it doesn't add up."

"Okay. Hang on to the journal for now. See if you can get any more out of it. Just, please, don't lose it."

I tightened my mouth. He made it sound like I did that a lot.

"If you find something, let me know, and as soon as you can."

Batting a thousand, aren't you, Wyatt?

"Ricky? Any word on that ring?"

"Nope. Mike says it'll take a few days to research it."

"All right. Let me know when you hear from him." He flipped his legal pad closed and threw his pen on top. "Okay, gang, let's get back to work."

I rolled my eyes. Like we hadn't already been working. I kept my eye on Ricky when we got back to our desks. He didn't seem to have any lingering guilt about his confession. I really wanted to ask him what kind of stuff his sister had on him, but held back.

The diary of Miranda Richards gnawed at my inner-snoop. I was over-thinking it, but something just Bugged. Me. About. It. As much as I'd mulled and mulched and spread, the same results kept coming up.

A light bulb went off.

The hearts! They must be a code. Or *could* be. Surely, she was cleverer than using them to mark when she was working. And, why hide it? She had no siblings; she was six when her mother died, and her father pretty much left her alone.

If the hearts meant a meet with a boyfriend, then her 'dates' had to be after she was done babysitting. That meant late-late nights. Would her 'older' man patiently wait at her house until the mayor brought her home?

No, I couldn't see that. And Mac wouldn't have tolerated it.

Then, inspiration. Well, not really. Kind of confirmed my own theory that this was a decoy, a diversion. It *had* to be a smoke screen. She was trying to throw someone off track.

But who?

If we could get into Miranda's room, again, I had a pretty good idea where exactly to look. All those shoeboxes. Somewhere, in one of them, was the real diary of Miranda Annabelle Richards, in all its X-rated glory. The county hadn't been looking for that kind of thing. They might have gone through the boxes, but had probably overlooked the little book.

By quitting time, I was more tired and cranky than usual, most likely from using all my brainpower trying to figure out that blasted red herring, and not thinking about other stuff. Whatever the cause, facing an empty icebox wasn't high on my fun things TO-DO list for the evening.

Annetta's Diner had a great supper menu.

The place was about empty when I walked in, and it was a surprise to again have Annetta seat me, and in the same back-booth Wyatt and I'd shared for our noontime the day before. She handed me a menu before bustling away to somewhere else. Left me wondering why she'd stuck me way in the back, but didn't mind.

A few minutes later, she returned, leaning against the edge of the table, snapping her gum. In her pink waitress uniform, with the frilly white apron, and never-fading carrot-red hair swung up into a beehive, she reminded me of Flo, from the old TV classic *Alice*.

Oh, come on, *Early to bed, early to rise* ... you remember that show.

"How come you're taking orders on this side of the counter?"

She gave a laugh and a wave. "Evey said she was going to be a little late. I'm just filling in for the kid."

"Evey Peters? Cody's kid-sister?"

She nodded, and blew a bubble.

"Really? I didn't know she was working here."

"Oh, yeah. Been here about.... Well, I'll be. Been almost a year, already. Kinda strange, how that all came about, I recall. Sailed in one day, all in a hurry-like, and asked if she could help out in the afternoons. I said sure, as Susie had just quit to work at Sporelli's."

"Susie Chapin? That was sudden, wasn't it? I remember her being in here on my late lunch runs. I thought she enjoyed her job."

"Thought so, too. One day she comes in and says, 'Today's my last day.' Didn't give any more notice than that. So, there I am, stuck with no suppertime waitress, and no possible replacement on such short notice. How lucky is it that Evey comes in the next day? Ya ask me, they worked it out that way, and on purpose, too."

"You think so?"

She nodded. "Had to've. And when we got word about Miranda, you'da thought Evey was her best friend, the way she carried on. Had to take the night off. Yeah, she was real shook up over Miranda's death."

"Do tell."

"Yup." She pulled out her little order pad and clicked her pen. "What'll ya have tonight? A whole meal, or just coffee and pie?"

"Oh, Annetta, you're sly." Laughter. "I'll have the country ham dinner, with sweet tea. When I'm done with that, I'll let you know if I have room for dessert."

"Sure. Comin' right up." She grinned and went to yell my order at her son, the chef school graduate short order cook.

I hauled my purse onto the table and began to rummage for my book. No, not the novel-of-the-moment. Crosswords help me pass the time while waiting for my meal to arrive, other than twiddle my thumbs … which doesn't really help. Puzzles are relaxing, the way knitting is for others.

Why not bring a book? Funny you should ask. Because usually I get irrationally aggravated at the waitress for interrupting me, or so absorbed in the story my meal gets cold. So, no. Hard and fast rule, no reading at the table … whether it's in a restaurant, or at home.

My bag must weigh fifteen pounds or more—

probably an exaggeration as it hasn't ever been weighed. Not sure why that is—not that I haven't weighed it, but that it's so heavy—there's nothing that heavy in it, and I *do* clean it out once a week. You'd think it would be lighter, but no.

Slowly, my arm and shoulder muscles are developing definition from lugging the silly thing everywhere I go. If someone ever gets a notion to attack me, it wouldn't take but one swing, right upside the head—*Ka Bam*—and the perp'd be out cold.

By the time Annetta came back with my tea, I'd found my crossword book and was hunting for a pen.

"I've been meaning to talk to you," she said out of the corner of her mouth. "I know y'all are investigating Miranda's death. Have you interviewed everyone?"

I set aside my puzzle book. "Annetta, you know I can't—"

She waved at me, irritated. "I know that. What I meant was…. Oh, never mind. I'll just come right out with it." She slid into the other side of the booth and inched her nose close. "The mayor's been actin' real strange since this business with Miranda. Well, actually, since before then, but it's gotten worse. You do know she was their babysitter, don'tcha?"

"We do. Yes."

"Well, if you haven't talked to them, you need to. I'd do it separate, myself. That way they can't co'oberate their stories."

"Them?"

"The Pattersons. Mayor and Mrs."

I laughed. "Thanks for the advice, but we've got it

covered." I took a sip of the sweet cold drink. "Why do you think they shouldn't corroborate their stories?"

She lowered her voice and peeked around. "I don't wanna get in trouble for this."

"Don't worry, Annetta. I'm not going to broadcast it. And if I repeat it to anyone, it'd only be Wyatt and Ricky."

Satisfied she continued in a stage whisper. "Okay. Well, I'm not exactly sure why I feel so strongly about this, but I think Mayor Patterson's acting too fishy to not be involved somehow. And, I don't believe for a minute that Miranda killed herself."

I sat back in my seat and studied her. "Me, either."

"Because, number one she wasn't depressed, and number two her car wasn't where she was found. That means that *someone*," she stabbed a fork into the table, "drove it away from there."

My brows raised, impressed that she knew so much about it. "Annetta, you should have gone into law enforcement." I was going to ask how she found out about the car, but she started talking again.

"Thanks." Another fork stab. "But that's not all. He comes in here a lot. When he does, he stares at Evey. Has for as long as she's been here. I didn't put it together at first, but then I remembered that he used to do the same thing when Susie worked here. She acted half-afraid of him most of the time. Now, he's doing the same thing to Evey.

"And his behavior is odd while he's in here, too; not just the staring thing. I can't really explain what I mean, just that he doesn't act the same as he used to.

He's worse." She stopped to look over her shoulder. "Always seemed friendly. Had a good word for the customers who were in here at the time. Now, though, he slinks in the door, not a word to anyone, and he sits as far in the back as he can get. No smile, no hello, or anything. The 'friendly' he does show is almost inappropriate, and it's mostly aimed at my part-time help—all high school girls." She shook her index finger at me. "I see how they react to *him*, too. Flattered that the handsome mayor is paying attention to them, but intimidated when he gets too touchy-feely. And, he *does* get touchy-feely. Not overt to the point of X-rated or anything, but just shy of inappropriate." She shifted closer. "How do you say 'back off' to the mayor? Ya know?

"Now, Miranda was their babysitter, and it's no secret that he took her home every time she sat for them. But he was up to no good, if you ask me."

The picture forming in my head made me queasy.

"Have you seen him lately ... like, in the last few days?" She closed her eyes and shuddered before continuing. "Ever since Ricky found Miranda, the mayor's been a mess. His face is gaunt and gray, hollow-eyed. Short-tempered. Complains about the service or the food, or whatever.

"I'm telling youz, Maggie, something bad happened. And it happened *because* of him, or *to* him, or both. And, I think it's connected to Miranda's death."

I wanted more details, but a little bell jingled.

Annetta straightened, and stood up like someone jabbed her in the ass with a pin.

"Oh. Your food. Hang on. Be right back." She

hurried to get my plate.

Pretty spry for an almost fifty-year-old woman who's been wearing out pairs of shoes all day for the past twenty years or so. Wait! What am I saying? She's not that much older than me.

The puzzle book had lost its appeal and was returned to my bag. Annetta had effectively taken up my excess minutes, and imparted some very attention-grabbing stuff, too. Stuff that needed to be gone over in my head a second time, and studied ... thought about.

Stuff Wyatt needed to hear.

Especially her concerns about our *distinguished* mayor. Hadn't seen the main man in a while, so I couldn't judge his mood or appearance. Wyatt was supposed to question him in the next few days.

Oh, calamity and hardship. I was going to have to break down and call the chief of police at home. Had to remember not to forget to tell him about the fake diary, too. Yeah, I'd already told him and Ricky my theory, but we needed to find out for sure if there was a real one. He'd told me to let him know if I thought of anything else ... as soon as possible. This qualified. Didn't it?

"Here ya go, Maggie." Annetta's chirpy voice brought back my focus as she set my ham, mashed potatoes, and carrots down, along with two homemade—still steaming—biscuits, with a side of honey butter.

Mouth-watering.

"This looks great, Annetta. Thank Wally for me, will ya?"

"Sure. Need anything else?"

"Nope. I'm good. But, listen…." My knife slid smooth and easy through the juicy inch-thick piece of meat. "If you want to talk some more, let me know."

"Thanks. I will." She looked up as the bell over the door jangled. "Oops, got a customer. I'll be back to check on you shortly. Enjoy."

"Mmm, definitely." I took a bite of ham.

CHAPTER THIRTEEN

AFTER PAYING THE check and leaving my friend a nice tip, I went to my car. A turn of the key … a few clicks. Another turn—nothing. Rolling my eyes at Gertrude's stubbornness, I turned off the key and pumped the gas … just once—she's a mature Plymouth—then tried again. She wanted to, my poor Gertie, but she didn't start. I couldn't chance flooding her, so I sat there for a couple minutes. Okay, so I was thinking evil thoughts about her, but I didn't say them out loud. She wouldn't have started at all, if I had.

Five minutes later, I tried again, and just like that, she started without any protest. "Must've been a fluke, right, Gert?" I patted the dash, and pulled out of my space.

All the way home, I thought about what Annetta had told me, even the weird stuff about Susie and Evey. Did it all tie together? Susie had graduated two years before, but I couldn't remember if Evey was in *her* class, the next class, or Miranda's. What would connect the dots? Would those dots tie those three girls together? What about Annetta's ramblings? Was the mayor really involved up to the hairs of his chinny-chin-chin?

"I wonder." I bit my lip and tried to hurry Gertie around the next corner. Getting home quick was a priority in order to make notes - so I wouldn't forget my brilliant idea. That happened a lot lately—my forgetting things.

Don't talk to me about old age, I'm only, um, forty-something, remember?

I hit the garage remote and up the drive we went. Gertrude slid right into her slot without a fuss. "Gertie," I said, in my most persuasive voice as I gathered up my belongings. "You had better get a good night's sleep, so you can start right up in the morning." I closed my door and walked around the front bumper. "I can't afford to have you clunk out whenever you feel like it. If you're sick, we'll have to take you to the car doctor, again. You like Dodge Peters, don't you? He's always treated you very well. But, I need you, little girl."

Oh, hush. If people can talk to their plants, I can talk to my car.

I unlocked the connecting door to the house and went in, leaving Gertrude alone to do her cool down *tick-tick-tick*.

My bag thunked onto the kitchen counter and I stood with my hand on it. What was it I was supposed to remember? "Oh, crud." I went to my desk in the hallway for a tablet and pen. "Come on, think. What was that light-bulb-moment idea you had in the car, Maggie Lou?" It did no good to stare at the blank sheet of paper. Neither did growling. "I can't remember." I hate when that happens. Making a fist almost broke the pen in half.

The tablet went flying across the room, pages flapping like an injured pelican. I stomped down the hall, needing to change into my comfy-clothes - lounger pants and an oversized T-shirt—compliments of my oldest son. I liked it; he lost it. Unpinning the

French twist, I brushed out the kinks, and banded my long hair into a tail.

I'm one of those female anti-establishmentarians who don't believe that once you hit your mid-forties—*oops*, did I just admit that?—you have to chop off your hair to your earlobes. If my grandmother, and those before her, wore it long and up in a bun, why shouldn't I? Well, not in a bun, but you get my drift.

I went to the kitchen. It was time to take care of me, to relieve some stress, to bake. It was a trait. Not a medically recognized inherited one—like blue eyes—but more of a 'hand-me-down' compulsion, from my mom and hers. Growing up, all the sibs and cousins knew when there was something major happening in the family because there were baking sheets, batter bowls, and lots and lots of cookies everywhere. And thank the Lord for dishwashers!

While gathering ingredients, I ping-ponged about calling Wyatt. Two trays of aroma-filled, nicely golden, chocolate chip cookies later, it was decided. Munching one, I made a pot of coffee, then dialed the boss. I'd never done that before—called him at home.

"Hey, it's me." My mouth was full of cookie. "Are you busy?"

"Um, no. What's wrong? Somebody tape your mouth shut?"

I frowned and swallowed my mouthful. "No. Listen, I had supper at Annetta's—"

"Really?" Laughter. "Is the food as good at suppertime as it is at lunch?"

"Um, yeah. She, uh, she told me some things that could impact the case. Made me feel weird, too.

Interesting … disturbing things you need to know about. Could you…. *Would* you, mind coming over? I really think we need to talk about them tonight."

"Hmm."

"If you'd rather wait until tomorrow, that's fine, too." The oven timer went off. "Oh, crud. Hold on a sec." The receiver clunked to the counter as I raced for the hot pads. Cookie baking was an exact science, more or less, and it only took an extra minute for them to be *too* done. The baked tray got swapped for an unbaked, and the timer reset. Once the hot tray was on a cooling rack, I went back to the phone. "Sorry about that. So, do you have time for a discussion tonight, or—"

"You're baking cookies." It wasn't a question. Actually, it sounded like an accusation.

I cleared my throat and looked around at the mess in my kitchen. "Um, yeah. I am."

"What kind?"

"Right now? Chocolate chip." I frowned at the phone. Was that a moan, or a whimper? "Wyatt, are you okay?"

"Got coffee?"

I looked over at the pot. "Um, yeah. Just finished perking."

"Be there in ten."

ARGH! He didn't even wait for me to say good-bye before hanging up.

True to his word, Wyatt arrived as promised, pounding on the back door like somebody was chasing him. Opening it, I glared … I hoped it was a glare. "Good thing I didn't have a cake in the oven."

"You ought to be arrested for baking cookies

without inviting someone to share." He glared back as he shouldered past me into the kitchen, where he inhaled deeply.

I *shoo-shooed* him and went over to the coffee pot. "I would have brought them in to work in the morning." I poured two mugs.

"Yeah, and Ricky'd have 'em all eaten before I got there. Besides, they wouldn't be fresh-baked-hot-out-of-the-oven gooey, in the morning."

I shrugged. "That's not my fault. If you didn't take all day to get to work…." I set the cups on the table.

Ignoring me, he made himself at home, getting the milk for his coffee out of the refrigerator, then taking a seat in front of the pile of cookies. "Okay. Tell me." He bit in. A moan escaped, and his eyes rolled back. "Maggie, you have to marry me. I can't stand the thought of you marrying anyone else. I would never get any more cookies, especially fresh baked, like this."

My hands went to my hips. "I didn't bake them for you." What was I saying … the man just proposed MARRIAGE.

He started on his second cookie as I took another pan out of the oven. He'd said marriage.

"If I promise to say you're the best cook in the county, will you save yourself for me? I mean, cookie baking-wise?"

I laughed and shook my head—and, my God, Wyatt had said *marriage*. "Sorry, Dude. Ricky would die of starvation."

"Who's more important?" He grabbed a third. "Oh, man. On second thought, never mind. I'd look like the Goodyear Blimp if I ate like this all the time."

I put a pout on my face. "You mean you don't want to get married, after all?"

He stared over the edge of the half-eaten chocolate chip cookie. I bit my lip. He was way too solemn. "When I get serious about it, Magdalena, I won't be asking because of your baking skills."

Oh. There he went using my whole name again … got me all tingly. And, he'd said *when* not *if*.

Lord, have mercy.

I used a potholder for a fan, and wished I could stare anywhere but at the man munching away at my confectionary creations.

Now y'all get your minds out of the gutter. This is primetime, after all.

However; getting back to business, those little niggles in my belly, those were real, not my imagination. Wyatt was definitely interested.

Double WOW!

He took a swig of coffee and smiled … the one that makes me melt into the floor. "Come sit down. Tell me what's got you all worked up."

I almost laughed; almost said, *Besides you?* Instead, I refilled our mugs and sat across from him. "Okay. You know I had dinner at Annetta's." He nodded. "According to her…."

I recounted everything the woman said, even her theories about Susie and Evey. "I just have this weird feeling that something, or someone, somehow connects those two girls with Miranda. Not that they had anything to do with her death, but whatever it is, it's making my skin itch."

Wyatt reached across the table and grabbed my

hands. I gasped at the contact. "Maggie, you're ruining that cloth, and it's a very nice one. Calm down."

I lowered my eyes and saw that I'd been picking at the frayed edges of the dishtowel on which the cookies were cooling. A small pile of fuzz and threads lay next to it on the table. "Guess I've been stressing."

He laughed. "I could tell that by the mountain of sweets you've baked."

"Am I that transparent?" The timer went off again, and I got up to retrieve the tray. There wasn't another one prepared to go in, so I turned off the oven. My momentum was gone.

Ya gotta have a routine, ya know? A pattern … like an assembly line. Wyatt was a big distraction, but talking about Annetta's suspicions had thrown me even further off track. I sat down again, bit into a cookie, and with a grimace, laid it aside. If I ate anymore, I'd be sick.

"Have I told you how good these are?" Wyatt devoured another one.

Now, that was odd. "Not in so many words, no, but I got the gist." Eyeing him over my coffee cup, I wondered where he was going with the flattery.

"Are you going to bring any of these to the office tomorrow?"

Hmm. "If there's any left after you get finished. If I don't, they'll just tempt me and I'll have to eat them myself." *And that's not going to happen.* "That will take too long, and they'll start to get crumbly and dry … and then I'll have to throw them out."

He tensed. "Um, that won't be necessary. Ricky

and I will handle the rest. You won't have to … throw them out. Can't have them go to waste like that."

"Wyatt?"

"Hmm?"

He looked innocent, but I could tell there was something going on behind those big beautiful browns. "All that sugar is going to your head. What's going on?"

"Not a thing."

Definitely too innocent.

Okay, two could play at this game. "Do you think Annetta's concerns have any merit?"

He stopped chewing mid-cookie. It took him a minute to answer. I could almost see the gears shifting. "Uh, I don't know. Randy's death affected everyone—and certainly me. If she was the mayor's exclusive babysitter, he may be truly grieving. If Annetta has something solid … you know, as in, evidence … I can get a warrant. Otherwise, I'd be an embarrassment to the uniform, and this town, if I show up at the mayor's office and arrest him just because we have a concerned citizen who thinks he's guilty of something. As for the two girls...." He shrugged. "We could bring them in for questioning, or go visit them at home."

I shook my head. "I can't imagine the mayor involved with any of this, let alone Susie and Evey. I haven't seen Ridge in a while, though. That in itself is strange. He usually stops in a couple three times a week."

"I'll have a talk with Annetta. Maybe she'll have something to add to what she told you. Some people are like that, you know. They tell me something one day and the next they're back, because they remembered even more." He stopped and picked up another cookie. "Getting back to these things here." He waved it at me. "You have a secret recipe, right? Are you part witch, or something? These things are— I can't stop eating them."

"Sure you can. You only have another dozen or so more to go before they'll be all gone and you won't have any more to eat. And, no, there's no secret formula—unless you count the fact that I use semi-sweet chips instead of milk chocolate. I just follow the recipe on the back of the Toll House chocolate chip package." I squinted at him. "I figured it out."

He raised his eyebrows. "What? Figured what out?"

"I know what you're doing."

"What am I doing?"

"You're going to rub it in Ricky's face that you got hot-out-of-the-oven cookies, and he didn't. Right? Am I right? I'm right."

He leaned back in his chair and laughed. "You really are a witch."

"Nothing paranormal about it. I'm just that good." I gave him the *smug-mug* look. "I'm right, aren't I?"

"I should go." He got to his feet. "Looks like you have some more baking to do. I'll get out of here and let you get to it. We'll bring Ricky up to speed tomorrow. I have no doubt he'll enjoy questioning those two young females."

I pursed my lips. He sure was in an awful big hurry all of the sudden. Was it something I said? "Huh. You're right. He probably will. Probably have to take each one out to dinner, to discuss things." I waved a hand at the counter. "But, I'm not going to bake anymore tonight. I'll just cover the dough and stick it in the fridge. Tomorrow night'll be soon enough to finish up."

"Sure you won't need any help?"

"That's not help, that's elimination."

He took his mug to the sink and held his ... flat stomach. "Man, I'm gonna have to run two extra miles tomorrow morning, but I wouldn't have missed it for the world. Thanks for inviting me."

"Technically, I didn't invite you, not for cookies. They were just subconscious motivators."

"Aha. I knew there was something psychological about it. Either way, I appreciate the cookies, and the info." He moved to the door; I followed. "Sleep well. I'll see you in the morning."

I watched from the doorway as he walked out to his Jeep, then waved as he drove away. He hadn't acted mad, or upset, but the mood had shifted dramatically. Or was it just my imagination?

My sigh wasn't sad, not exactly. It would have been so nice ... so absolutely fantastic ... if he would've-could've stayed longer, lingered over coffee, gazed longingly into my eyes, whispered sweet nothings.... Sorry, there I go again—cliché-city, and I don't care.

Alas.

And whose fault was it that he hadn't? Mine, for not speaking up and telling him he's.... What? The love of my life? The conversation hadn't moved in that direction and I hadn't steered it that way. The fear of rejection (or outright laughter) kept my wishing all in my head and heart. It wasn't a matter of one-sidedness anymore, but how serious was he? Yes, he flirted. Does he flirt the same way with every woman?

Sheesh, he better not.

Thinking about him teasing Vicki Sporelli made my belly hurt.

Was he just as wary as me about a relationship? Do we both want the same thing, but keep dancing around it too fast for it to catch up with us? All of the above? Or, none, because of my vivid, fantasy-laden imagination.

The aggravation made me want to punch something.

It's hard enough to build a romantic foundation with someone when there aren't any distractions. Being in the middle of a murder investigation was more than that.

"Oh, for the love of Pete! I forgot about the diary!"

CHAPTER FOURTEEN

FRIDAY....

THE CHOCOLATE CHIP cookies waited inside a pink cardboard Corsair's donut box next to the coffeepot. Wyatt might be too full from last night. Ricky might not care for cookies.

Yeah, right.

One or the other better show up soon, I was getting antsy. It's hard to look busy when you're not, and don't want to be obvious about it.

"Hey, Maggie." Ricky greeted me tiredly. This case was wearing everyone out.

"Good morning, Officer Anderson." Maybe I should have been reading, like I normally would be.

He made his way over and took a big whiff of Maxwell House, then moved to the small table and lifted the lid.

At the long lack of sound, I stopped pretending not to look.

He stood, eyeballing the open box, his mouth open and slack.

"Ricky, if you drool on those cookies, I'm gonna have to hurt you." He could eat the whole box, for all I cared. I'd had more than enough last night. Just the smell kinda had my stomach roiling.

Knowing Ricky, though, I wouldn't put it past him to mark the lot so no one else could have any.

He closed his mouth, but continued to loom over

the tempting fare. "Those are chocolate chip cookies."

"Yup."

"Homemade?"

"Yup."

"Yours?" He looked over his shoulder.

"Yup."

A momentary pause. "How fresh?"

"Last night."

He whimpered.

I frowned. The sound was similar to the one I'd heard from Wyatt the night before. "What is it with you guys and chocolate chip cookies?"

"Us guys? What us? I'm the only one here." He turned around, grinning evilly, and rubbed his hands together. "I could touch them all. Then Wyatt wouldn't get any."

See there? He just made my point.

"That's all right, he—" I bit my tongue. Uh oh. Shoot shoot shoot. If Ricky found out about last night, things could get ugly.

He lost the grin. "He what?"

"Nothing. Aren't you going to have a cookie?"

He wasn't about to be distracted. "Don't change the subject. He what?"

I closed my eyes and mentally smacked myself in the head. And, as luck would have it, the subject of our discussion chose that moment to make his appearance.

"Mornin', Maggie." He smiled at me as he removed his hat, then looked over at his young cohort. "Ricky. Hey, watcha got there?"

As if he didn't know.

I didn't bother to return his greeting.

Stone-faced, Ricky looked at him, then me.

When Wyatt got close enough to see into the box Ricky hadn't closed, he grinned. "Hey, great, you brought the cookies. They were so fantastic last night, right as they came out of the oven, all hot and gooey." He slapped the kid's shoulder. "You shoulda been there, man."

Ricky's burning gaze pinned me to my seat as he answered. "Well, I would've been, if someone had bothered to call and in-vite me."

I wanted to hide under my desk. No, I wanted to clobber Wyatt over the head. He was a good one for smacking at a beehive just to see if he could get something to come out.

Then came 'the mad.'

I didn't have to put up with this. We weren't even blood kin. And, they were acting like....

"You two are acting like three-year-olds." I got to my feet. "From now on, if you want any sweets in this office, bring your own." I grabbed my purse and stalked out the front door with as much dignity as I could muster.

Yeah, it was probably dumb of me to walk out. But, you know what? There's only so much macho posturing we gals can take. I'd reached my limit. It wasn't a blistering mad, only a mom-mad. Like when two brothers are constantly going at it, and you just want to clunk their heads together to knock the stupid out of them. I'd never actually tried it. Don't think it would've worked if I had. Males are so … hard-headedly aggravating, with their petty competitiveness.

With no particular destination in mind, as it was a spur-of-the-moment thing, I decided to have a quiet cup of coffee at Annetta's. The first corner booth next to the window was empty.

"Mornin', Miz Mercer," a soft voice greeted.

"Evey Peters. Hello. I heard you were working here. Thought you worked the afternoon shift?"

She smiled. "Coffee?" At my nod, she sat a mug on the table and filled it with fragrant dark-brown brew. "Yeah. Normally I work three to eleven, but Annetta asked if I'd work mornings for a few days. You know, to see if I like it. So far, it's pretty great. I have to get up a lot earlier, but it's not as hectic as the later shift."

"Good. I'm glad. Liking your job helps—a lot. So does liking the people you work with."

"You're right about that. Working with Annetta's a blast. Will you be wantin' some breakfast?"

"Nope. Just the coffee. Thanks."

She smiled again and walked to the next table.

Maybe I needed to take my own words to heart. But, I did like the people—okay, the men—I worked with. Sometimes, though, all that testosterone tended to get overpowering. The lone-female syndrome could have advantages, but there were also disadvantages. And, even though I'd been in a similar situation while married and raising two rambunctious boys, I wasn't immune.

There was something else bothering me, too. The Rapunzel in the tower … of my brain … was pouting about why Prince Charming hadn't followed and made it all better? Well, yeah, why hadn't he?

Guess you're not worth it, Maggie Lou. So much

for mutual interest.

I brooded until my cup was empty and went to pay for it. Pity Party was over. Time for damage control.

When I got back to the station, Ricky's patrol car was gone. At least I'd only have one Neanderthal to deal   with.

CHAPTER FIFTEEN

AS IT TURNED out, Wyatt was gone, too. Hands went to hips. "They didn't even lock up. Must've been pissed, or figured I'd be back real quick." I shrugged, sat, and began type-type-typing up my reports.

About fifteen minutes later, hats in hand, they came up to my desk. I tilted my head and glared … waiting.

Ricky moved over a little and pulled a big bouquet of flowers from behind his back. "Sorry, Maggie."

The kid's smile was a bit crooked, and the red was creeping up under his collar. He was going to make someone an adorable hubby.

I folded my arms over my chest, trying to hang on to my irritation. "I've been mad at you guys before and you never brought me flowers. What's the deal?"

Wyatt answered. "For one thing, you never yelled at us and left before. This whole week's been hectic enough without us … me, adding to it. You've been putting up with a lot from everyone in town."

"We also figured, maybe, it would put some points in the plus column … since we took advantage of you—unintentionally, of course—you know, with the donut thing. And that, maybe, you'd forgive us and keep bringing cookies and donuts and whatever, to work in the mornings?" There was hope in Ricky's voice. "Pretty please?"

I sighed. Now how could I stay mad? "So, in other words, this is a bribe?"

They grinned.

Ricky shoved the bunch of blossoms at me. "Is it working?"

"Of course. But what am I going to do with these?" I reached for the fragrant spray. "I don't have anything to put them in."

"Not to worry." Wyatt held out a large cut-glass vase.

"Oh." Tears sprung. "You guys. Thank you."

They elbowed each other.

"Told ya." Ricky's whisper wasn't quiet.

I laid the blooms on the desk and stood to take the vase. "Don't push your luck." I used my mom-voice.

They cleared their throats, and hurried to their separate office areas.

Secretly more elated than I wanted to show, I went to get water. Guess I was worth it. Take that alter ego.

Later that morning, out of the corner of my eye, I saw Wyatt come out of his office and make his way towards me. I glanced up and stopped typing. "What's wrong?"

"I need a favor." He sat on the corner of my desk, but there was nothing flirty about his mood.

"Okay. What?"

"Actually, it's for Mac."

"Oh?"

"He asked— He needs…." Wyatt ran a hand through his hair, then crossed his arms and bowed his head.

I almost laid my hand on his thigh. "What does he need, Wyatt?"

"He needs someone to help him pick out something for Miranda … to wear." He shook his head. "He's not dealing well."

Didn't sound like Wyatt was, either. My heart went out to both. "I understand completely. I had to do that when my Bernie died; it's harder than you might think. When does he need me?"

"Apparently, the funeral home's been calling, and he's been putting it off. I guess that means, as soon as you can get there."

"Okay." This was serious stuff. I saved the report on the computer and closed the file, then reached under the desk for the tote bag I call my purse.

"Would you like me to drive you?"

Was that hope I'd heard?

I straightened and stood … too fast. My head spun, and I had to lean on the desk to wait 'til the stars disappeared. "That might not be a bad idea. Would you mind?" I wanted to smack myself in the head. Idiot. "Forget it. Don't answer that. Stupid question. Did you offer because you want to keep me company, or because you want to be there for Mac, in case he needs support? Or both?"

He blinked, and I cringed at how dumb all that sounded. Then, he smiled and grabbed my arm. "Come on, let's go."

I guess he was going to drive me over there

without giving me an answer.

Mac was on the porch when we got there, hands in his pockets, leaning against the railing, looking like he was the one ready to go in the ground. I got out of the car, walked up to the man, and put my arms around him, again. Instantly, he engulfed me in a bear hug. All I could hear was the tearing agony of a father's grief as he bawled on my shoulder, again.

"Mac. I'm so, so sorry." Rubbing his back, I tried to comfort him, but cried along instead. I didn't realize Wyatt was so close, until I heard him blow his nose.

Mac must have become aware of how exposed we all were, out on the porch like that, because he took a deep breath before letting go and wiping his eyes on his shirtsleeve.

"Thanks for coming." His voice was raw. "Come on in. I still can't go in her room. If you could just pick out something pretty for her to wear, I'd appreciate it, a lot." At that, again, the tears started rolling—for both of us.

Latching onto his arm, I led him towards the front door. "Let's go. I'll see what I can find." I glanced over my shoulder and reached out my other hand. Wyatt grabbed it like a drowning man, and we all went into the house.

"You know which room is hers." Mac gestured toward the staircase.

I had my foot on the first step when my brain flashed a question. "Mac, how did she get to be the babysitter for the Patterson's?"

He mopped his eyes and blew his nose. "Not real sure. She told me the school secretary had some kind of list."

"Thanks, Mac." I leaned over and patted an arm. "I'll have to give her a call. You sure you're not coming up?"

He shook his head. "Her favorite outfit was hip-hugger jeans and one of those little stretchy tops that showed off her belly button. But, I'd like something dressy." He was trying keep control. "I don't even know if she has anything like that."

I rubbed his arm, felt his anguish, but resolved to be strong. "Don't worry, Mac." I started up the stairs. "I'll find something."

"Thanks, you guys. Don't know what I'd do without you."

Taking over, Wyatt led him into the living room while I continued to the second floor.

This would be the perfect opportunity to go through her closet. Now I wouldn't need to talk to Wyatt about coming back. Just one more box checked off of my To Do list.

I groaned, disgusted with my own analogy.

It felt strange—kinda creepy, actually—to be amongst her clothes and shoes, again.

My first priority was finding an appropriate outfit. Mac wanted pretty. There was an aqua blue dress at the far end of the closet. Didn't look like she'd ever worn it.

Do they put underwear on corpses? I couldn't remember, so I picked through her delicates and placed a bra and panties on the bed, next to the dress.

Now, for the shoes. She certainly had an extensive selection. On the floor, among those lined up two-by-two, was a full two-row rack, plus stacks of boxes against the wall. I went through each carton, since none of the displayed shoes seemed to be the perfect pair.

In my search, I discovered they didn't all contain footwear. My active imagination had been spot-on. Some held secret treasures she'd collected, and in one, near the very bottom of the stack in the corner,

JACKPOT.

Another diary.

Although I'd hoped I was right about the first one being a red herring, I hadn't been actively searching for a real one, hadn't gotten that far, yet. Now, here it was, practically dropped in my lap. An exact replica of the first one—pink with a locking clasp. A Little Miss Secret. This one, she hadn't bothered to lock.

How weird was that?

A quick flip-through told me the dates were about the same as the diary we already had. I mentally pumped my fist in the air. I'd been right about the decoy.

"Did you find everything?"

CHAPTER SIXTEEN

I LET OUT a shriek at the unexpected sound of Wyatt's voice just behind my left shoulder. "Geez, Wyatt. You almost scared the color outta my hair."

"Sorry, thought you heard me."

I had a hand on my chest, to hold my heart in place. I'm not sure why people try to do that … it's not like it actually does any good. I waved in the direction of the bed. "Yes. I did find everything, thank you. What do you think of the dress? Is this pretty enough, plain, or too bright?"

"No. I think it's perfect. Do you have shoes?"

"A closetful." I held up the white sandals that had been in the box with the little book. "These will look nice, I think."

"They look new." He paused. "You do realize it's going to be a closed casket, don't you?"

I gave no answer. There was no need. Instead, I promised: Randy, you're going to look great, top to bottom.

"What else did you find?" He lifted his chin towards the shoeboxes.

I peeked over his shoulder, to make sure Mac wasn't nearby. "I founnd another diary. It has the same dates as the one we already have."

His face showed approval. "Excellent detective work, Miss Marple." He picked up my purse from the floor near the door, where I'd set it upon entering this room of secrets, memories, and grief. "Stick it in here."

"Good idea." I dropped it inside.

"You ready to go?"

"Think so." I laid my hand on his arm. "I should remember this, but I don't. Do they put underwear on dead bodies?"

He shrugged. "No idea. I don't think it matters, does it?"

"I'll take it, anyway … just in case."

Downstairs, when Mac saw the dress and shoes, he started in again. I felt miserable for making him cry, but of course, it had nothing to do with me. I knew that.

Holding the outfit close to his chest, he thanked us again, and Wyatt ushered me—quickly—out of the house. If he was feeling like me, he wanted to stay and help, but couldn't wait to leave. In the car, the macho man remained very quiet.

I stared out the window. "I'm going to have to make some casseroles to take over."

"Casseroles? Why?"

"So he eats, and because I can't bring his girl back, and because that's what we do, and because…. Just because. If he doesn't have to bother making a meal for himself, just heat up a dish, he's more likely to actually eat."

We were sitting at the longest red light in Mossy Creek proper. "Why don't you offer to make casseroles for me?"

Turning, I gave him the look. He couldn't be that dense. Not about funeral protocol. Could he? "Wyatt—"

"I'm sure I'd enjoy your cooking, but I don't want anyone to die in order to get any."

I gave him a light shove. "You devoured the chocolate chip cookies I made. Wasn't that enough? Is this a sideways invitation for me to cook?"

"Not nearly. Some might call it sideways begging. Is it going to work?"

I reigned in a laugh. "All you have to do is ask."

"Okay." Wyatt faced forward and starting breathing in and out in long measured strides—What the …—then he said, "Magdalena Elizabeth Susannah Maria-Louise Mercer, would you cook a meal for me? Sometime?"

My jaw dropped, eyes went wide, and I may have forgotten to breathe.

Good Lord! He knows my name.

Did he realize what a big deal that was, that he knew the whole entire thing? That he'd gotten them all in the right order?

"Maggie? You okay?"

Am I okay?

No. Not really. I closed my mouth, and swallowed, hard. Major plus points to him, that's for sure. Wow! "Maybe. I think. You're serious."

"I'm seriously thinking about what maybe means. Doesn't have to be a casserole, unless that's what you want to make."

"Uh. Okay. When?"

The light finally went green, and he gave me a quick glance before proceeding through the intersection. "We should probably wait 'til after the case is done. I'll let you know."

I gave a nod. Probably couldn't have formed a sentence, anyway. Wyatt was a man of many mysteries, and I was liking every one that unveiled.

"Excellent. Thank you. I already know how good your cookies are. I can't wait to taste … your cooking."

I heard that slight pause at the end and got a hot flash. Heavens to Betsy, and her three twin sisters. What was I getting myself into? Who cares? Whatever it was, it was fun.

We pulled into the station parking lot and Wyatt put the SUV in park. Turning off the engine, he sat back and looked over.

I looked back. Waited. He obviously had something else on his mind. If I waited long enough, he'd eventually decide to talk, maybe.

"Why'd you ask Mac about the babysitting thing?"

"Why? I can go along, but I can't ask questions?" I hoped he wasn't going to get technical, or tell me I couldn't because I'm not official law enforcement personnel. I'd been thinking about accepting that honorary peacekeeper badge the council had offered. Another topic for us to discuss, at some point.

"Yes, I mean no. You asked him if he knew how Miranda found out the Patterson's needed a babysitter. Did you have a specific reason for asking?"

I shrugged. "I was curious. Usually if someone needs a babysitter, they call around to their friends, to find out who they'd recommend. In this case, I doubt the mayor had many friends to ask; his wife either, for that matter, since they hadn't lived here all their lives. Was Miranda a volunteer? Did the Pattersons go through the phone book?

"And, how long was she their babysitter? Since

Kendall was born? Or, more recently? Her diary, the fake one, has hearts around—" I gasped, realizing what I was figuring out as I said it. "Shoot." I smacked myself in the head. "Her first diary, it's a calendar! It should tell me when she started working for them. Maybe it will tell me if she knew—or when she suspected—she was pregnant." I frowned, talking mostly to myself. "It won't tell me how she got to be their sitter, though."

Wyatt was looking confused and I almost laughed. He shook his head and unbuckled his seatbelt.

I grabbed his arm. "Do you know the high school secretary?"

He shook his head again, this time in answer to my question, and got out of the vehicle. I wrinkled my nose in annoyance, and fumbled for my seatbelt. Wyatt opened my door as I freed myself. "I don't know her name." He stood in front of me. "But Ricky may have already talked to her. If not, she should still be at the school. The staff usually has stuff going on for a week or two after classes let out. You could call her."

I turned sideways on the seat—my knees touching his belt—and grinned. "Thank you, Wyatt."

He took a deep breath—like he needed air real bad—and stepped back. "You're welcome." He waited until I was clear before he shut the door and hit the remote lock. "May I suggest that you secure that second diary in the evidence locker for the time being?"

"You don't want me to go through it?"

"Not right now."

"All right." Confused, I capitulated—he was the police chief, after all—but I didn't like it.

I would have thought, with so few leads to go on, he'd want to know anything Miranda had to say. Especially in case she named her killer. But, I should have known he had more to say. I opened my mouth to voice my protest, but he beat me to it.

"On second thought, right now, we need to have a short meeting with Ricky, and then I want you to go home and lock yourself in with that thing. I want to know everything that's in it, backwards and forwards. We're gonna be really busy, especially at the funeral tomorrow. I'd like to tell you to wait 'til next week to go through it, but we don't have that luxury." He paused again. I began to wonder if he was trying to use telepathy as a viable means of communication.

"Now, don't take this the wrong way. Make sure that piece of evidence isn't left lying around unprotected, even in a drawer. Something might happen to it."

What did he think I was, an idiot? "I get it, Police Chief Madison." I started past him.

"I don't think you do." He stopped me with a hand on my arm, before I got too far ahead. "Forsythia Morgan has been making daily visits to the office after you leave in the afternoons. I don't want our best lead to be accidentally misplaced … if you know what I mean."

My jaw dropped. Second time in ten minutes. "She's been coming in after I leave? Whatever for?"

He shrugged. "Haven't the foggiest. Fishing. I don't even know what she's talking about half the time. She's on this bad-mouthing kick. I call it bad-mouthing. Stupid gossip, tattle-tailing, really, about people doing things for which she thinks they need to be brought to justice."

"Oh, for Heaven's sake. This all has to do with that Vera-Mae Wellington deal, doesn't it?"

He nodded. "I'm thinking."

"Sorry, I did take it wrong. I'll lock up everything on my desk, especially if she's going to be lurking around."

"Magdalena?"

I blinked. There he went again with the name-thing. I rubbed at the goose bumps peppering my arms. "Yes, Wyatt?"

"About that, um, meal?"

I stared, waiting.

"I've been really hungry for some homemade lasagna. If you've a mind to make it, I'd be very appreciative."

I smiled, a little wicked. "How appreciative?"

He grinned and wiggled his eyebrows. "Very."

I wrinkled my nose. "That's no answer."

"Let's just say, I'm sure you'll enjoy the benefits of my appreciation."

"Will I?"

"Very much."

"You are such a tease, Wyatt Madison."

He laughed. "Don't get me started."

What a concept.

Once inside and settled, I snagged Ricky before he left on a call. According to him, the secretary, one Evelyn Forbes, had made sure Miranda's teachers were available for him, but had been away from her desk the day he went to conduct the interviews. I called the high school and was relieved when the woman answered the phone. The Pattersons had called her for recommendations. The mayor suggested she ask a few of the senior girls if they would be interested. She'd made a list of three or four she thought would do a good job, and called each one into the office. After deliberating over their qualifications, she'd decided on three for a list. One primary and two backups.

"They were satisfied with your choice?"

"Very much so. Well, I say that because they only called once for one of the backups, or a different sitter. "

"How long ago...? How long have you been providing a senior girl to the Pattersons?"

"Since little Kendall was six months old. That was," I heard papers rustling, "2006."

"I see. And each new school year, they've requested a new sitter?"

"Well, they didn't really request one. I assumed, because the sitter from the previous year had graduated, that they would require ... well, that they would need another senior."

"Hmm. He wasn't upset, or disappointed, or anything?"

"Oh, no. They both seemed quite happy with my choices."

"Who actually made the initial request?

"Oh, Mayor Patterson. He and his wife had discussed it, he said. My suggestion of the senior class seemed to please them. He did suggest not adding any boys to the list. Said a senior girl would be more responsible, and probably have more experience."

"Gotcha. So, how many have babysitted … ah, babysat, for the Pattersons?"

"Well, just three. Three years. Three different girls."

"May I have their names, please?"

"Sure. First was, let's see, Susie Chapin. The next year was Evey Peters. And, unfortunately, this year was Miranda Richards."

My Martian antennae went up. "Really? How very interesting."

"Yes. Well, actually, it was a little odd."

"Odd?"

"Yes. This year, at least. The Friday before school ended, the mayor called for a backup girl. He'd never done that before. He had a banquet that evening, and didn't want to use Miranda anymore. I asked him why, since there had been no complaints up to that point. But just wanted a change, he said. Being such short notice, I told him I couldn't guarantee that the backup would be free. He said he didn't care, that he wanted someone else.

"I called each of the two backup girls, and neither of them could make it. I hated to call Miranda, because he'd said they wouldn't be using her again, but there was no one else to call. Miranda was very confused, and a little angry, because she'd already been planning to sit for them."

Then a low sound, like she wasn't sure she should say anything more.

"And then—and I don't know if this is connected—but I had a call from Evey Peters, this past Wednesday. She said I shouldn't recommend any more girls to the mayor. I didn't really understand why, although, if I had a suspicious mind…. But that would be, well, that's just sick."

I didn't comment, could hardly catch my breath. Good Lord. No wonder the mayor stared so hard at Evey and Susie. Annetta had been onto something big. "Thank you, Miz Forbes." I hurried her. "You've been a great help. I appreciate your talking to me." Hanging up, I slouched back in my chair, stunned. We definitely had to talk to those two girls, pronto. And, I needed to let Wyatt know what I had found out.

"What'd she have to say?"

"AAH!" I jerked so hard I nearly fell off the chair; my heart jumped, too, into race mode for several seconds. "For Pete's Sake, Wyatt. What's the deal, sneaking up on a person so deep in thought? That's twice today you almost gave me a heart attack."

"Sorry, thought you knew I was there." He'd parked himself on the other end of my L-shaped desk. I twisted in my chair to look at him. He leaned forward, until we were almost touching noses. "Besides, I think you've got a very healthy heart."

"Thank you." I answered automatically. It took another second for his comment to sink in. Whoa. I needed to not think about that, for the moment. Had to shove it to the back of my brain, and only bring it out when I had more time to analyze it.

I rolled my chair away, about six inches. Right now, I had to focus on the new information I'd collected. "How soon is Ricky going to be back?" I sounded winded.

"He should be walking through that door any

second."

"He should hear this, too. Can you wait that long?"

"Long as you need." He stood.

My top teeth grabbed a lip, and I briefly closed my eyes. Heat bloomed.

He'd stopped being subtle; maybe he never had been. Maybe I'd been too dense to see it. Either way, the box was open. No way was it getting shut again.

He nodded, as though he could read my thoughts. "When he gets here, come on back."

An hour later, after I relayed all I'd learned from Evelyn Forbes, and my opinions on what I thought it meant, my two comrades were just as flabbergasted.

CHAPTER SEVENTEEN
FRIDAY, EARLY AFTERNOON....

JUST AFTER LUNCH, I was startled again when the front door banged open. Obviously, I wasn't going to leave as early as Wyatt intended. The diary was burning a hole in my purse, figuratively, of course, at my feet.

Vera-Mae Wellington sailed—or rather, it looked as though she wanted to, but hampered by the ace bandage still wound around her leg, all she could do was limp heavily—into the room.

She stopped in front of my desk, the whole of her short slim body vibrating with anger. She shook the copy of The Mossy Creek Gazette clenched in her out-stretched fist. "How could you, Magdalena Donovan? How could you embarrass me like this? You had no right."

Wow. She must be even more upset than it looked like. I hadn't been a Donovan since I married Bernie, almost thirty years ago. Not knowing what she was ranting about though, I waited to see if she explained herself before deciding whether or not to be angry. I did stand and wave to a chair. "Sit down, if you please, Miz Wellington, and we'll talk about what's bothering you."

The dark purpling of her face was causing me some concern.

She squinted, her mouth all scrunched up as if

she'd eaten a really sour lemon. "Don't patronize me, young lady."

"I wasn't trying to. I'm trying to get you to sit down before you fall over and break a hip."

She smacked at my arm with the newspaper. "Oh, don't give me that."

My brows shot up. "Then, how about: I don't want you to have a heart attack in front of my desk?"

She harrumphed. "I'm as healthy as a horse. You're stalling."

"Miz Wellington, I honestly don't have any idea what you're talking about. Please, sit down and calm yourself. How'd you get here, anyway?"

"I drove."

"Thought you weren't supposed to drive with your leg all banged up."

"I'm well aware of that, thank you, but I was just so darned furious." She sat with a thump, aggravation radiating in waves. "Goodness, now I'm cussing, to boot."

I bit my lip to keep from smiling at her definition of a curse word. "What are you so het up about?"

Her eyes bored.

My eyebrows went up, again.

"You … you blabbing your mouth about my mint juleps. What I do in my own house, is my own business. You had no right—"

"Hold it." I held up my hand, shocked at her words. I was getting angry. "What are you talking about? I don't blab my mouth."

Her eyes narrowed even more. "Don't you read the paper?"

"Actually, no. Not if I can help it. Why?"

"Read today's headline." She thrust the badly crumbled paper at me.

I sat down and smoothed it out, then sucked in a breath as I silently read said headline, and the article beneath. TEETOTALING TEACHER TIPSY. Uh oh. She may be retired, but Miss Vera-Mae Wellington is still a respected leader of the community. However, this reporter has learned through diligent research, and a reliable source, that the distinguished former educator spends her evenings sipping fermented spirits.

"Oh, dear. Oh, Miz Wellington. This is terrible." I scanned the byline and was even more appalled. I studied the beleaguered woman in front of me. Should I sympathize first, or be irritated that she thought so badly of me? I crossed my fingers and went for a midway approach.

"First of all," I began. "I'm as shocked by this as you are. Second…." I shook my finger. "I'm mad at you. Do you really think I'd stoop so low as to tell anyone what you said to me in confidence? What would I have to gain from it? Did you even notice who wrote this piece of trash?"

She had her mouth open to speak, but only shook her head. I guess I shocked her with my 'mom' voice.

"Forsythia Morgan, that's who. Why on earth Owen Harris hired her as a reporter is beyond me. But, tell me, Miz Wellington, just who would have been her reliable source? And, what kind of research would she have had to do, to get that kind of information?"

The woman groaned and covered her face.

"Yes." I nodded at her, though she couldn't see

me just then. "You should be ashamed. Forsythia did come here, right after you left the other day, and tried to pump me for information. But, I didn't tell her anything. I wouldn't be much of a police dispatcher if I gossiped with the head of the grapevine, now would I? Besides, she's the one who mentioned the mint juleps. Sounds like the two of you have had some grand ol' times."

Vera-Mae lifted her head; red-rimmed watery blue eyes stared. "Why would she do something like that? We're supposed to be friends."

"Why does Forsythia Morgan do anything?" I shrugged, and all my anger dissipated.

Clutching her pocketbook, she took a breath. "Can I have her arrested?"

Sitting back in my chair, a smile tugged at my lips. "I don't know if it's legal, but we might be able to sweet talk the chief into making a very public 'token' arrest on say … libel?"

The woman's face brightened. "Really? Oh, that would be splendid, and so satisfying." She folded her hands in her lap. "Magdalena, I'm so very sorry. I'm so ashamed. I don't usually jump to conclusions so quickly."

What could I say? Forgive and forget. I waved away her apology. "Don't you worry about that, Miz Wellington. Why don't you put a little bug in the chief's ear, when he comes out to talk to you?" I took a good look at her. "Are you feeling all right, now? Your color's coming back."

She nodded, smiling. "I'm just fine, my dear. Thank you."

Once Miss Vera-Mae left, I was alone. Ricky was out questioning the last of Miranda's cheerleader squad and Wyatt was following up some loose ends of his own. Since I had to stick around until they came back, now would be a good time to dig into that new diary—barring any interruptions.

I retrieved the little book from the bottom of my bag and opened it.

March 7th: My first date as Kendall's babysitter is tomorrow night. I can't wait. Ridge Patterson is such a hunk. If he's as horny as Evey Peter's told me he was, I probably won't even have to talk him into it. I'd noticed him before, he is the mayor, of course, but the chance to make out with him is so … wow. Makes me wet just thinking of the possibilities. Danny's pissed because I told him he's not mature enough for me. Sure, the sex was great, but he's such a clinging … hee hee … Klingon … yeah, that's it. Can't breathe when Ridge's around me.

March 8th: Ridge made a point of driving me to and from his house. Insisted on it, even. What a rush. On the way back, he stopped on Foggy Bottom Road. My heart started pounding. As soon as he turned off the car, I slid over the seat, up against him, and kissed him, hard. He sure was surprised. Guess he liked it, a lot, because he started kissing me right back, and grabbed my boobs. What a dork. But then, he started rubbing my—

"Hey, Maggie."

I gasped and jerked; the diary flew to the floor. Holy hot potatoes! Took a few slow deep breaths to calm down. My heart sure was getting a workout. I bent to pick up that steamy little volume. "Ricky, you scared me near to death."

He was grinning, like he knew and had done it on purpose. "Wyatt around?"

I swallowed. "No. Why?"

"I'm gonna run out to the lake and look around."

"Oh?"

"Yeah. Saw Dodge a minute ago. Says he saw the mayor Sunday, around noon. Watched him take off from The Corner Grocer's, and head down Skunk Hollow Road toward the lake."

I nodded. "I'll let Wyatt know when he gets back."

"Shouldn't take more'n an hour and a half, tops."

I saluted as he went out the door. Good grief. Wondering if I was ready to tackle more of Miranda's triple-X passages, I got up for a bottle of water. If all else failed, I could pour it over my head.

By the time Wyatt and Ricky returned, I needed an industrial strength fan and a cold shower ... or two. And, there was more to read! Holy Hannah-Banana.

Five minutes later, Wyatt called us to his office, feet propped on the corner of his desk. "Anything to report, Rick?"

"Yeah. I've got some news."

"Maggie?"

"Um, yeah. But, you better turn up the air conditioning before I give it."

Wyatt laughed. "I actually came up dry today. So, Rick, you go first. Whatcha got?"

"Nothing new from the rest of the cheerleader squad; didn't really expect there to be. They're, uh, no offense, Maggie, but they're pretty ditzy. Didn't know anything. Didn't see anything. Didn't really want to. That kind of attitude. Hate that."

"Why apologize to me? Besides, not every cheerleader is like that, Ricky." I wanted to defend them, but as I'd never been one—mainly because most, even in my day (shh), acted like brainless Barbies—I didn't have much to back it up with. Mind you, I didn't say they were brainless, just that they acted like it.

"Oh, I know. When I played football, there were a couple of girls on the squad that were okay."

"So, why don't you look them up and ask them out?"

Ricky opened his mouth to answer, but the boss interrupted. "Could we make dates after work, please?"

"Sorry, Wyatt." Ricky sent me a mind-your-own-business look and went back to his report. "Anyways. I was on my way back, when Dodge Peters stopped me. Sunday he saw the mayor comin' out of The Corner Grocer's with a couple a six packs. Looked spooked about somethin'. Didn't say a word, though, just got in his car and took off down Skunk Hollow Road … toward the lake. I drove out there and looked around. Unless he cleaned up his own empties, the maintenance people must've policed everything." He looked up from his notes. "You said Mac was out there. Maybe he saw 'im."

"Now, that's good stuff, Rick. I'll give Mac a call in a minute, see what he has to say." Wyatt swung his feet to the floor and leaned on the desk with his elbows. "Anything else?"

Ricky shook his head.

"All right. Maggie?"

I wrinkled my nose. "Maybe you want to call Mac first."

"Because?"

"Because, what I have to report might, well, it's…. Just call Mac."

Wyatt complied without comment, which surprised me. "Mac, question. When you were out at the lake last week, did you happen to see Mayor Patterson?" His eyebrows rose. "Really. Oh, yeah? And then went to his car for another two? Huh." He picked up a pen, slid his legal pad closer, and began to scribble. "I see. Thanks, Mac. I appreciate that." He closed his eyes. "Yeah. I know, Mac. I'll try to get there today. All right? Yeah. Okay. Thanks again. Bye."

Ricky fiddled with his pen. "He was there? On Sunday?"

"Yes. He was there, with four six packs. Must have been saving up. Drank twelve bottles, then went and got another two sixes out of his trunk. Mac said he acted like he was upset about something, and didn't want company. Even offered the man the use of his porch, but Ridge went and sat on the dock to drink. Tried to keep an eye on him. Didn't want him falling in."

"Which means?"

"Which means: the mayor has an alibi for

———

Sunday."

"Did Mac happen to mention what time he saw the mayor?"

"Says it was just after lunch when he got there, but that the man was still downing brews after dark."

"What was the coroner's time of death?"

He flipped open the file at his elbow. "Sunday, 9:45 PM."

Ricky frowned. "But, the mayor's still a suspect."

"Everybody's a suspect."

"You're sure Mac saw him on Sunday?"

Wyatt leaned back in his chair and studied the rookie. "Rick, you're the one who told us Dodge saw him with two six packs."

"Yeah. Yeah, I did." He ran his hands over his stubby hair.

From Wyatt: "So, what's the problem?"

"I don't know. It just feels … wrong."

"Let's table it for now. Maggie, your turn."

UGH. I slung the pink journal across the table. Ricky caught it as it passed. "You might need some oven mitts." I warned him.

"Yeah?" Wyatt kept his attention on his notes, but looked amused.

"That hot, huh?" Ricky poked the corner of it with his finger, then shook it, like the book'd burned him.

"Worse than some of those romance novels I used to read."

"Trashy?"

"Course not. I don't read trash … didn't … don't." I sniffed. "Erotic."

"Oh. 'Scuse me," Ricky laughed. "Erotic."

Wyatt looked up from the file, mischief on his

face. "You read those things?"

"Not anymore." I fanned my face, sure it was beet red. I'd actually forgotten how arousing those novels could get, 'til I read Miranda's blow-by-blow.

Stop snickering.

Her narrative.

Oh for Pete's sake, not you too?

Wyatt's "too bad" had me fighting a grin of my own.

CHAPTER EIGHTEEN

RICKY WAGGED HIS head. "I can't believe you read stuff like that. You're a mom, for Cripes sake. Mom's aren't supposed to be interested in that kind of thing."

"If we weren't interested in 'that kind of thing', we wouldn't get to be moms."

Wyatt snorted. Ricky's neck went crimson.

I ignored them both. "I'll tell you one thing, she was sure this one wasn't going to get read by anyone but her. Wow. Talk about explicit. There are things about the mayor I never ever wanted to know." I pointed to the book. "Disgusting. I wish I hadn't read it, but boy, does it paint a different picture of Miranda and Mayor Patterson."

Ricky wiggled his eyebrows. "Oh, yeah? Like what?"

"Aha. See? You shouldn't need to read that kind of stuff, either. You're … um, probably…. You don't need … uh, any help—crud. Never mind." I groaned. "I'll bet that's why you read your sister's diary. You wanted to know all the juicy stuff she wrote about."

Wyatt smothered a laugh when Ricky's jaw dropped. "Geez, Maggie. She was only ten. There ain't no juice at ten … least-wise there shouldn't oughta be."

I rolled my eyes. "Ten? You made it sound like she was in high school."

"See what happens when you read too much

Fabio."

"I read romance, even erotic romance, but no, not Fabio."

Laughter.

Wyatt jerked his chin. "Are you gonna tell us anything, or just tease us along?"

"Oh for pity's sake. All right. After the first couple times they broke the speed limit, he told her that as soon as she graduated, he was going to divorce Ellie and marry her. How sad is that? She assured him she was on the pill, and he stopped using condoms. Eeeuw. But she lied, she wasn't on the pill. She got bunned-in-the-oven on purpose."

Ricky made a face. "You're right. That's way more stuff than I needed to know."

"Yeah, well, that's mild. She describes, in detail, what they did together. How it felt. How, even though he was an incredible lover—like she had so much experience in that area—she felt guilty about deceiving Ellie."

"Not guilty enough to stop," Ricky commented.

"No. I don't think the mayor knew about the baby, maybe not until Saturday night. As far as I've read, she hasn't mentioned telling him yet, and I have no doubt that if she had, she would have written it down. The when, the where, the how, and his reaction."

Wyatt bopped his pen against the table. "If it was Saturday night, that would explain why he was so upset on Sunday."

"Exactly." I shook my head. "Please, Wyatt. Don't make me read the rest. I don't think I can handle anymore."

Ricky chortled. "Ooh ooh, poor Maggie. You can read trashy fiction, but not the real thing?"

"I don't read them anymore," I protested, but it sounded lame, even to me. "Besides, it's not the same. Not the same, at all."

Wyatt broke in. "You haven't read the whole thing?"

"I just said I didn't. I only got to the end of May."

"Sorry, but I really need you to read the rest of it. We need to know what's in there. Did she write about anyone other than the mayor?"

"Yeah. Thankfully, not in the same context."

"You mean like being with an older, married man." Snap! Wyatt's pen now lay in two. "Whatever. Maybe, just maybe, she gave us a clue to her killer. Please, Maggie? For me? Read the rest of it?"

I narrowed my eyes. "You don't know what you're asking. You really don't."

"Then give it to Ricky. Perhaps he can be more objective."

"No, Wyatt, it's fine. I'll finish it."

"Hey! I can be objective."

"Shut up, Rick. Maggie's already deep in it, and this way, we won't have to tread over old ground."

Silence.

Wyatt looked at me, smiled, swept his broken pen into the trash can, and said: "Thanks, Maggie, this means a lot."

I twisted my mouth. "Well, you did insist."

He flipped the file shut. "Rick, tomorrow morning, after the funeral, take a ride over to The Corner Grocer's. Talk to Al, or whoever was on duty last Sunday. Get all the info you can. That's it, I think we're done."

Ricky made a note in his little book, nodding.

We all stood.

"Oh wait, one more thing. We should meet out in the parking lot in the morning and go to the funeral together. A show of force, if you will. Could be beneficial. Is 9:30 good for both of you?"

We nodded.

His reasoning was sound, but really, I knew Wyatt just wanted to have company—our company. God knew he wasn't looking forward to the service. He couldn't grieve there, would have to stand tall - be the man the town saw him as, needed him to be. There was still a killer loose so when others cried, they'd need to turn and see Wyatt, see the man. Well, it would be a show of force; Ricky, myself, and our chief, a promise to everyone present that justice would be served—and on a friggin' platter.

I dragged myself out to the parking lot and into my car, feeling like I'd been wrung through a wringer. All I wanted was to get home, change into my comfy stuff, and flake out on the couch. No baking for me tonight, too tired even for that.

Besides, I had to read the rest of the diary, and make copious notes, for Heaven's Sake.

CHAPTER NINETEEN
FRIDAY, LATE AFTERNOON....

GERTRUDE WAS HOT and sticky inside, but I knew once I cranked her up, she'd cool down quick. I stuck the key in the ignition and turned it, already anticipating the frigid air I'd feel after a minute or so.

All I got was a whine. So, I did some of my own. "Come on, Gertie. We talked about this last night. Remember? I thought we agreed you weren't going to act up anymore?"

Sweaty, I tried again, moisture trickled between my fingers, making the key slippery. This time there was a grunt, but no turnover. I pumped the gas … once. "Obviously you weren't listening, missy. Please?" I tried, one more time.

"Don't ignore meee."

A click ...

… just a little itty bitty gritty …

… shi—"My-car's-not-starting-for-meee."

Click.

By this time, my clothes were soaked, and droplets were dripping through my hair and down my face. Growling, vicious and long, I pounded the steering wheel with both fists, then leaned back against the headrest and counted to ten—by threes!

"Well, Gertie, I guess it's time to let you go to into the light. You've been a great help to me for twelve years, but lately you've been letting me down.

You've cost me over a grand in repairs in the last month alone, and who knows what's wrong with you this time. And, now, I have to find another way home."

I wasn't looking forward to making monthly payments again, but this automobile had gone to the great car lot in the sky.

Pulling the keys from the ignition, I got out of the car with a groan. It was actually cooler outside. One of my boys would have to come rescue their mother, again. Not that they wouldn't drop everything and come get me, they would, without question.

I trudged into the front office, just as Wyatt turned off his light.

He looked up, eyes wide in surprise, and … was that pleasure? "Maggie. Thought you'd gone home."

I wiped a damp sleeve across my forehead. "That was the plan, but my car had other ideas. It won't start. I came back in to call for a ride."

He stood twirling his hat. "I'll take you home."

My handbag thunked on the desk. "Oh, no. That's okay. One of my boys will come get me." Why was I protesting? My alter ego wondered the same thing, mentally smacking me upside the head—whapwhapwhap. I must be nuts to turn down a ride home … with him.

"Why should they have to disrupt their evening when I'm already here?"

He sounded so logical.

I hesitated. I couldn't let him think I was too easy. Could I? Hah! "Well, okay. But I don't want to put you out." Yeah, right. Snicker snicker.

"It's no trouble. Really."

I gave him a look. "You live on the other side of town."

"Magdalena." He stepped closer and stopped spinning his hat. We were almost touching. "Would you please allow me to drive you home?"

I swallowed. How could one refuse such a gallant offer? "Um, okay."

He took hold of an elbow. "Let's go." He opened the door.

Grabbing up my bag, I went out to his Jeep Cherokee and watched as he secured the building. He then came around to unlock and open the passenger side. I did the shy upward glance-thing, unable to hide a smile. "Thanks." He nodded and I got in. As he shut the door and went around to his side, I realized he was nervous.

The ride to my house was both too long and too short. He pulled into the driveway, turned off the vehicle and got out, circling around to open my door.

Wow. Chivalry is definitely alive and kicking.

I slid out, and he walked me up onto the little front step. My keys were still in my hand, so I didn't have to hunt through my purse for them. Good thing. He took them, unlocked my door, and handed them back.

Then, he did the even more unexpected. He took my face in his hands, leaned close and said, "Maggie, I've been needing to do this for some time now. If you feel the need to slap me afterwards, I'll understand."

Then he kissed me.

OH! Puddle on the porch stoop!

It wasn't a quick peck-kiss either; it was a soft,

moist, slow, ooh ooh ooh, yummy yummy, give-me-more, kiss.

Slap his face? Are you kidding? Returning his kiss was a thought one second, and an act the next. My purse hit the deck. I slid my hands around his waist and up his back, angling my head for better access to his mouth. I heard a moan. Was it him, or me?

Ask me if I care.

He stopped first. Well, not all at once. He kept teasing me with little sips and slurps, until finally resting his forehead against mine; having as much trouble breathing as I was. "I guess you're not gonna slug me." He was holding me snug against his chest.

"Um, no," I assured him, enjoying … savoring, the closeness. It felt really good squashed up against him.

"Good. I was going to wait until this case closed, but in all good conscience, I just couldn't do it. You're becoming way too important to me, Magdalena. Like I said, I was going to wait, but damn, woman, I just had to taste you. After sampling your cookies, I couldn't wait to kiss you. Should have done it before I left last night, but I might not have been able to make myself go home."

I was speechless. "I've been, um, hoping this would happen for a long time, too. I wasn't sure how you felt about me."

"Soooo, this something you'd like to pursue more thoroughly?"

I leaned away and smiled. "You betcha. Most thoroughly."

He grinned. "Excellent. I'd like to start out with a

traditional date, if you don't mind. I don't know if it'll work out that way, though. Would you have dinner with me Saturday evening?"

My smile got wider and I felt my heart laugh. "Absolutely. What time?"

"Six-ish? Casual, dressy."

I tilted my head. "Is that a question, or a statement?"

"Statement."

"Which translates to, dress or slacks, no jeans?"

"Right."

"Mmm, K. Looking forward to it."

He grinned again, and captured my mouth for another hot kiss. "Me, too."

When I was able to focus again, he'd already gotten in the Jeep, and was backing out of the drive. I gave him a wave and went into my house all flustered, closed and locked the door, then rolled my eyes.

I reopened the door, snatched my purse off the stoop, and locked up again.

Standing in the middle of my living room, a hand on my chest, I tried to get my breath back to normal and keep my jig-dancing heart inside my body. "Dandy! Where are you when I need you, girl? I have a date with Wyatt Madison! On Saturday night!" Two spins and I was dizzy. "Eat your heart out, Vicki Sporelli."

I giggled like a five year old with a new doll, then froze and let out a horrified gasp. "Oh, my stars and garters. That's tomorrow night!"

CHAPTER TWENTY
SATURDAY, MORNING....

I WOKE UP groggy and grouchy. Wyatt's kiss had rattled me more than it should have. And, to top it off, the contents of the diary only fired up my already humming libido. Goodness. My face was still pink-tinged this morning.

Needless to say, I didn't get much sleep. Awake past two, getting hot and bothered by that … that racy bit of, fiction-like tripe—except that it was much too real—about too many people I knew personally. Then, tossing and turning the rest of the morning with visions of what I'd read, super-imposed with Wyatt and me as the main characters.

Today was going to be very busy, and very long.

I shuffled into the kitchen, yawning while I made coffee, and almost fell asleep again waiting for it to brew. When the machine growled, I perked up and grabbed a mug from the cupboard. Not waiting for the beep, I poured a cup and took it to the fridge for a shot of milk, before taking a sip. "Oh, man, that's good." Sipped it all the way down the hall and into the bathroom. After one last swallow, I turned on the shower, disrobed, and stepped under the steaming waterfall.

By the time I dried off, the clock told me to hurry. From experience, I knew that the old saying, haste makes waste, was true. If I wasn't careful, my sheer black hose would have a run, my zipper would refuse to close, or I'd snag the brush in my hair.

There wasn't much black in my wardrobe, but I did have a suit that would work: a sleeveless sheath with a little black and white—herringbone style—bolero jacket that went over it. A short black sweater instead of the jacket would work out even better.

Thank goodness I hadn't gained any hip lately—credit due to my restraint against the daily donuts—so the size twelve had some wiggle room, just the way it should.

Way to go Maggie Lou.

The two-inch heels on my black pumps put me at five-ten, still a good six inches shorter than Wyatt. The concept gave me a pleasant rush.

I wound my hair into a little more sophisticated twist in the back, and secured it with a fancy black jeweled clip, then sprayed the heck out of it, and dared it to come loose. Just a smidgen of makeup, a little shadow and eyeliner with the mascara, a faint bit of blush, and some plum lipstick.

Finally, I felt ready and peeked at the clock. It was steady at 8:45. I'd made it, what a relief. I snagged my purse and went to the inside door to the garage, hitting the automatic opener I'd installed near the light switch. Then, I stopped and stared at the empty bay.

"Shoot," I yelled … to no one. "Shoot, shoot, shoot." I refrained from kicking the wall, and went back into the kitchen. As the connecting door slammed shut, my phone rang.

"Now what?" I wasn't in the mood to talk to anyone, but counted to ten before answering … on the third ring. "Hello."

"Good morning, Magdalena." A sexy baritone vibrated in my ear.

I smiled, my bad mood melted. "Good morning, Wyatt." I was surprised at how husky my voice had gotten so quickly.

"I figured since your car is still in the parking lot, you might want a ride."

I rolled my eyes. He remembered. Figures. "That would be excellent. Thank you so much for thinking of me."

He chuckled; it was deep and did oddly delicious things to my body. "Baby, I've been thinking about you all night."

Oh, man. I had to cross my legs as a wave of sensation rolled over me. All he had to do was talk to me and I was mush. Speech, at this moment, didn't seem feasible, let alone coherency. "Um, I had some trouble sleeping, myself."

I heard that rumble again and closed my eyes.

"Did you?" I could hear the smile. "Maybe there's something I can do, to help you sleep better?"

"Oh, oh, oh." Darn it all, that wasn't fair. Besides: "Wyatt, you can't say things like that to me."

"Sure I can. Look how stirred up you are. Makes things spicy. I like spicy. And you, Magdalena, you're the spiciest person I know."

"I was stirred up before you ever called," I groaned. "I'd like spicy a whole lot more, if I didn't have something depressing happening in an hour or so." His deep sigh came through the phone loud and clear and I could have kicked myself for ruining the mood. "I'm sorry, Wyatt."

"No. No, you're absolutely right, but I'm glad to know we're both on the same page. You're going to have to explain to me how you got so stirred up, so early. You ready to go?"

"Hah, yeah." I needed to ignore his persuasive tone. "I went out to get in the car, before I remembered my car wasn't there." Now why, in Heaven's name, did I blurt that out?

He laughed. "Be there in ten."

"I'll be here." That reminded me, I had to reclose the garage door.

"Can't wait to see you, Maggie."

"ARGH!" He'd done it again - hung up before I could say anything back. The clock read five 'til nine. After whacking the switch on the garage door, I went back through the hall and snatched a stack of tissues out of the box.

Never go to a funeral or a wedding, without tissues—it's an unwritten rule. Even if you don't like who's being buried or married.

Then I fidgeted. With images from the night before, and remnants of that hot little journal still jangling my nerves, I was not at all confident about how I, my body, was going to react with Wyatt in such close proximity. All the will power in the world was going to have to manifest itself … real quick-like.

All my fretting was for nothing. Well, not nothing, just temporarily delayed. He pulled in the drive and beeped his horn, for Heaven's sake.

Yeah, right, he can't wait to see me. I grabbed my purse and keys, and left by the front door, locking up before going out to his idling Jeep.

He jumped out and came around to open the door. He was wearing sunglasses, and that killer smile. "Hey, hey, Maggie."

"Hey, Wyatt." Then I looked at the rest of him, and frowned. "You're in uniform."

"Yeah. Technically, even though Miranda was my goddaughter and Mac's a friend of mine, I'm still on duty, and this is part of a murder investigation." He stood holding the door, staring at me. His smile got wider. "But, you look fine. Yes, you do. Very, very fine, indeed." He caught my hand, and helped me into the passenger seat. Which is not a small feat when wearing a narrow skirt. I settled in as he went around to his side.

I reached for my seatbelt, but he leaned across and got to it before I could.

"Allow me."

I bit back a whimper as his hushed tone sent a rash of goose bumps up my front. Oh, Lordy. How was I going to make it through this day?

He took his time buckling me in, and while he was so close, I closed my eyes and took a big whiff. Mmm. I bit my lip.

He sat back and put on his own belt, then looked over. I wished I could see his eyes. "You clean up good, Maggie. I like the makeup. You haven't worn it in a while. Course, I like you without it, too."

He started the Cherokee and pulled out of my drive.

I blinked. Every thought in my head just went … POOF! … into the twilight zone. How can he say something like that and be so calm? How do I respond? Could I respond? He makes me feel like a bowl of oatmeal—all hot and mushy—then expects me to speak like an adult?

"Maggie?"

I blinked again. "Yeah?"

"Is everything all right?"

See what I mean? No. I'm not all right. I have bats in my belly doing back flips. I can't form a single intelligent sentence. You're driving me crazy, you idiot man. But, I couldn't say any of that, not out loud. "I'm fine." Standard female response, specifically designed to pacify, I guess would be a good way to describe it, most of the opposite sex.

"Not having second thoughts, are you?"

"Second thoughts?"

"Yeah. About tonight."

He really didn't have a clue. If we didn't go out tonight, the insanity would be complete. The strain of it all would do me in. "No, not at all. I'm trying not to think about it too hard."

"What? Why not?"

"Wyatt." He could be so exasperating. "I'm so jazzed about tonight I can barely function. If I don't think about something else, I won't survive long enough to experience it. And reading that diary did not help. Not one little iota."

He chuckled. Hmm, sounded like relief. Figured he'd enjoy knowing that. "I'll try to stay civilized during the day. But tonight, look out."

"Yeah. That's kind of what I was afraid of."

Ricky, also in uniform, was leaned up against his Dodge Ram waiting when we braked in front of the office. Wyatt and I got into the department issue SUV, Ricky hopped in the back, and we took off for the funeral home.

The parking lot of Eshlemann's Funeral Parlor was all-but-overflowing by the time we pulled in. Wyatt parked in a VIP slot—because he was there in his official capacity—and we all got out. Ricky beat Wyatt to my door. We congregated in front of the vehicle.

Wyatt was doing the nervous-but-gotta-be-strong thing. I knew he was upset about not being there for Mac the way he wanted to, and having to hide all those feelings so he could be the law enforcement presence and maybe catch the bad guy.

I was edgy about the whole idea of a teenager being a casket, among other things.

"I'd like us to stay together, and in the back, if at all possible. Keep your eyes open for any and all odd behavior."

Ricky blew out a sharp breath and wagged his head. "This whole day's gonna be odd, y'ask me."

I squinted at him as we all started across the lot. He noticed and shrugged, but didn't elaborate. Inside the chapel, we signed our names in the guest book and sidled along the back wall behind the last pew.

I looked around. The atmosphere was thick and hushed. Off to the left, a skinny blonde woman in a navy blue suit was softly playing the organ. I didn't know her, so she was probably an out-of-town relative.

Up front, Miranda's casket of white and gold stood on a raised platform. An 8" x 10" of her high school graduation photo sat on top the closed lid.

That alone had me tearing up.

I didn't mention my subconsciously disturbing state of mind before because it was too hard to keep the images at bay. Staying busy was a huge priority so I wouldn't have to think. The reason I needed the distractions—what I couldn't bear to think about—was how I would come to grips with one of my boys being in that box. I couldn't bring myself to even briefly project the thought of it.

Miranda had been such a vibrant energetic young woman. Remembering that, my chest got tight. Superimposing one of my sons in her place … allowing just that much of a vision in … my heart jumped, then constricted painfully.

No. Stop. Don't go there.

Today was bad. It was hard to stem that horrible numbness—real and imagined. The squeezing anguish that comes out in uncontrollable groaning. I've known grief, but not like this.

This was agony.

When my husband died, yes, it was a deep raw wrenching of my heart, and I missed him terribly. But dealing with his death was different because his illness had lingered over a three year period. It's difficult to explain to someone who has never been a caregiver for any length of time, that what one feels—at the time of expiration—is almost relief.

To suddenly lose someone, as Mac had, especially at Miranda's tender age, and under these circumstances, was unimaginably devastating.

I honestly didn't know how he was able to stand it.

The sobbing in my heart nearly overpowered me. I fumbled for a few tissues from my purse when the first drops began to leak from my eyes. Wyatt moved behind me and I jumped a little when I felt him wrap his hands around my waist.

Whoa.

Why would he do that in this place?

But then, Ricky moved closer and took hold of my arm, leaning against me in a sort of sideways embrace, and I understood that they were both trying to comfort me. I don't know if either of them had a clue about what had me so upset, but I was grateful for their support. Never had it been more apparent how close the three of us were. Of course we were close, and I knew that, but never like this. They were my extended family. The hugs from 'my guys' effectively countered the cold dread and fear that had invaded my heart.

My birth-sons were safe.

I snuffled up the tears and dabbed my eyes clear as the service began.

Mac was a mess; the heart-breaking weeping, understandable. His sister and brother-in-law, and both sets of the grandparents, sat in the front row, there for support and comfort, but they weren't faring any better than he.

There wasn't an empty seat anywhere. Miranda's classmates, and fellow cheerleaders, crowded into the first several pews right behind the family, openly showed their grief.

The mayor and his wife were in the far corner.

She sat rigid. I stared. Her face, very out of character, was a mask of cold anger. Mayor Patterson bawled, unapologetically. His appearance was shocking. I'd never seen him so unkempt in public before.

Poking Ricky in the ribs, I jerked my chin at the two across the room. He looked at me and raised his eyebrows. The mayor was definitely not handling things well. His wife, even worse.

Reverend Blanchard, patient and solemn, concluded the service with a prayer, and everyone said, AMEN. "If there are any of you who would like to accompany us to the graveside, there will be a brief ceremony and prayer. At the conclusion, the ladies of the church have prepared a light luncheon buffet over at the church social hall. All are welcome to attend.

"We will dismiss by rows, and you may convey your last respects to Miranda Annabelle Richards, and extend your condolences to her family."

Mac, and everyone in the front row, stood and took their places next to the casket.

When the service moved to the gravesite, Wyatt again kept us in the back—it was easier to watch all the activity from there. This time, when he wrapped his arms around my waist, he pulled me back against his chest. It was very arousing, but I was frustrated, too, as if I were committing sacrilege. Here I was, getting turned-on at a funeral. How sick is that? I should be sad, somber. But I didn't make him let go.

"Thanks, Maggie."

Goose bumps whooshed down my arms at his voice in my ear. "For what?"

"For letting me hang on to you."

I gave his hands a squeeze and leaned my head

back under his chin. "You're welcome." Good thing I hadn't made a fuss.

The graveside service was a surprise. Not only was there no keening or wailing—except for the mayor—but, it was calm, peaceful even. As if, a relief.

Maybe it was. Perhaps now, with a sense of finality, Mac could relax. He did appear calmer, but one of his relatives may have given him something.

On the other hand, Ellie must have stayed in the car, or maybe she was hiding. A good thing, either way. Her husband was no less vocal than at the chapel. I was embarrassed for the man, and glad not to be anywhere near him.

Clark Kent - sorry, Danny Harris - and Bruce Prescott, his photog buddy, were on hand. I saw him nudge Bruce to get a picture of the weeping mayor. I could only cringe at the thought of tomorrow's headline.

Just as Rev. Blanchard ended the final prayer, Wyatt leaned forward and whispered in my ear, again.

I gasped as goose bumps covered me from head to toe.

"We won't be going to the luncheon. We need to get back to the office."

Disappointed, I wrinkled my nose—those ladies always put on a good spread—but nodded my assent.

He continued, "I can't wait for tonight, Magdalena."

 I bit my lip to hold back a whimper.

Anticipation was going to kill me.

CHAPTER TWENTY-ONE
SATURDAY, LATE MORNING....

BACK AT THE stationhouse, we gathered in Wyatt's office to go over our notes and discuss the case. Wyatt called the Patterson's, again. Obviously, they hadn't gone to the luncheon at the church hall, either. They agreed to a 2:30 PM appointment. What a surprise. After the way the mayor acted at the funeral, I didn't expect either one to consent, especially on such short notice.

"What'd you find out from Al?"

Ricky shook his head. "His place was all closed up for the day. Stopped by his house. Wife said he went fishing; left around five AM. She says he does that every few weeks, and he'll be back in the store tomorrow. I could take a ride out to the lake, if you'd like."

"No. Tomorrow morning will do. Well, guess that takes care of that for the moment." Wyatt leaned forward and pushed his coffee cup across the table. "Rick, would you mind getting me a refill?"

"No problem, boss." Ricky stood.

"One sec, though."

I looked at Wyatt.

He made eye contact, then focused on Ricky. "Before the grapevine has a chance to get rolling on this, I … we, want to give you a heads-up."

I tried to get his attention, but he ignored me.

Ricky shifted his stance. "What's up?"

Wyatt grabbed my hand. "Maggie and I are gonna start dating."

I blinked, and my jaw dropped. Wow. Cool. He'd made it official … and with our closest friend.

Ricky barked out a laugh and slapped his thigh. "'Bout time." Wyatt and I stared. He shrugged, grinning. "You two have been dancing around each other for months. Y'all finally came to your senses."

"You're not upset?"

"Upset? Gimme a break, Maggie. You're two of the best people I know. More like a mom and dad since my own moved to Florida. How could I be anything but happy for you?" He opened the office door. "One thing, though."

"Yes?"

He gave me a pointed look. "Ya gotta invite me over next time you make cookies."

Wyatt snorted. "Aw, quitcherbellyachin' and find your own girl. Your poor pitiful me act is wearing thin, bud. If she doesn't bake, send her over to Maggie's. I guarantee Maggie'll teach her right."

He got a wistful look on his face. "Yeah. Find my own girl. Wouldn't that be nice?"

"Oh, for Heaven's sake." I was such a sucker when it came to him. "Tell you what. Until you find her, I'll invite you—"

"Hey!"

"Shut up, Wyatt." I winked at Ricky. "Every once in a while."

"Thanks." He grinned and left the room.

Wyatt squeezed my hand, reminding me he still held it, and leaned forward to kiss my temple. "That was nice."

A shiver danced along my neck. "Yeah," I breathed. "I thought so. He's such a good catch. What's wrong with the girls in this town?"

"He'll find someone, in his own time. Maggie, about that peacekeepers badge."

I blinked. With his abrupt change of subject, my neural pathways paused, then switched lanes. "What about it?" I thought he'd told the borough I hadn't accepted it.

"I talked to a couple council members, in reference to our mutual concerns with the ... uh, flirting, etc."

"You what?" My face got hot. Lord, have mercy; he talked to the very people who could put the kibosh on ... whatever it was we'd started. To lay his job on the line, though; to confess that....

Even as my brain went spastic, the rest of me was secretly pleased. I guess he'd been more bummed about my reluctant refusal than he let on. Now wasn't that just something else?

"They gave their approval."

Oh, geez. "What, like, we have to have their permission to flirt with each other?"

"I guess." Obviously he didn't understand my irritation. "I took it to mean that neither of us would get fired for acting on our ... uh, attraction."

Well, when you put it that way. My insides started doing cartwheels, but I was still muzzy-headed. "You really think so?"

"That's how I'm taking it."

"That's good. I will, too, then. Thanks, Wyatt."

"Took effect immediately."

"So, like, right now?"

"Or, like from the day you got the letter."

"Seriously?"

Ricky came back in with the coffee. He looked at me and chuckled. "By that dazed expression she's wearing, I guess you told her?"

My eyes narrowed. "He was in on it, too?"

"I might have mentioned something about it."

"How long have you been keeping this to yourself?"

"He talked to me about it the day we ... well, the day we bought you those flowers."

They both grinned.

I sighed, outnumbered, out maneuvered, but happy.

"There's just one minor stipulation."

Silence.

Wyatt cleared his throat. "One of the members I spoke with was Roberto Sporelli. He 'suggested' he'd overlook the miniscule possibility of any fraternization, if we'd start buying donuts from his shop again."

"Excuse me?"

Ricky was looking too innocent. "Sounds like a bribe to me."

Wyatt's shoulders rolled. "He promised us a discount, but I told him there'd be no problem."

I laughed. Oh, how auspicious is that? I can smush it in Vicki's nose every morning!

An hour later, we were still in Wyatt's office talking over the case when we heard the front door open. Technically, we're all off duty on the weekends, but with the murder case unsolved, we'd

Jill S. Behe

been coming in every day. We weren't expecting visitors.

I got up to find out who had come in, and was surprised to see Susie and Evey. They stood nervously by the front door, heads together, whispering.

"Hello, ladies. What can I help you with?" I pulled Wyatt's door shut and went to stand at my desk.

Evey grabbed Susie's arm and propelled her in my direction. "Is the police chief in?"

"Yes."

"We'd like to speak with him, if we could, please, before we lose our nerve." She glanced at Susie.

I was about to ask them why, when Susie spoke up. "It has to do with, um, it might have to do with Randy's death."

"Wait right here for a minute, please." I went back to Wyatt's office and poked my head in. "Susie Chapin and Evey Peters are here to see the police chief."

I returned to the girls. "He'll be right out."

A moment later, he proved me right. "Ladies, how may I be of assistance?"

"There's something we, um, need to tell you," Susie said. "It may be related to Miranda's case."

Wyatt gestured toward the doorway where Ricky stood. "Why don't we have a seat in here, and you can tell us all about it."

The girls quickly glanced at each other, and both nodded.

We all sat around Wyatt's makeshift conference table, and a tape recorder was set up. Wyatt made it official. "The following are statements given by Susie Chapin and Evey Peters, on this twenty-first day of June, 2008, in the presence of Officer Ricky Anderson, Police Dispatcher Magdalena Mercer, and myself, Chief of Police Wyatt Madison. Who wants to go first?"

Evey said, "Susie, why don't you? It happened to you first."

"Um, okay. Well, it started about three years ago, in the middle of my senior year."

Wyatt interrupted her. "Excuse me, Susie. Would you clarify what year that was, please? For the record."

"Oh, sure. It was, um, January of 2006. We'd just gotten back from our Christmas break."

"That's great, Susie. Thank you."

"Sure. Well, the school secretary called me to the office. She told me the mayor and Mrs. Patterson were in the market for a babysitter—Kendall was about six months old by then—and she wanted to know if I'd be interested." She looked around at us. "Well, of course. Right? I mean, yeah, seventeen is getting on the old side of the babysitting thing, but I mean, it was The Mayor. Besides, I liked Ellie, I mean, Mrs. Patterson. And little Kendall was a doll. Totally adorable.

"The night of my first gig, Dad told me he'd drive me over, and to call when I was done. I could've driven, but we only had the one car, and with my mom so sick at the time, I didn't want to leave them without— Well, I mean, if there'd been a— If she'd...."

Evey laid her hand over her friend's. "It's okay,

Suz. They understand." She looked at us. "Right?"

We nodded.

For many years, her mother had been extremely ill: emphysema and a variety of other ailments. Hanging on by a thread during Susie's high school years, she'd died the winter after her daughter graduated.

The girl swallowed her grief. "Um, well, that first night, the Pattersons were back really late, I mean, it was after one in the morning. I asked to use the phone, you know, to call my dad, cuz, I mean, it would've been rude not too. The mayor said not to bother my dad, that he'd take me home.

"I said how I didn't wanna put him out, and he said it was no problem. I mean, really, getting a ride home with the mayor? Hey, I was somebody. My friends were gonna be so jealous. If I'd only known.

"Anyway, one night, about three months later— I'd just graduated, like, the week before, or something—we were on the way to my house, and he pulled onto Foggy Bottom Road ... there, where it meets Old Bear Creek Swamp? Thought he had a flat. When he didn't move, I asked what was wrong. He said he wanted to ask me something.

"I wasn't scared, but all of a sudden, it felt kinda creepy to be in the car with him, ya know? I didn't say anything. A couple minutes later, he asked if I thought he was cute. It was weird; I mean, shit, he's the mayor. What was I supposed to say? Right?

"I told him, sure, he was cute, for a mayor. Cuz, ya know, I mean, to me he was old, but not, like, ugly. He laughed and then leaned across the seat— real quick—and kissed me ... right on the mouth. I wanted to smack him. I mean, geez, he's married. And he's the mayor. He can't be doing stuff like that. What a jerk.

"But he wasn't done. He had to go and ask if I'd liked it. Can you believe that?" She shook her head. "I was sooo disgusted. I said no, that he shouldn't do it anymore, cuz, ya know, he was married and all, and I really liked his wife. He laughed again, and kissed me again—harder. Then, finally, he took me home.

"I thought that would be the end of it, hoped. For the next few weeks, every time he took me home, he'd stop. I was so scared. He'd kiss me a couple of times, then drive to my house.

"I never told anybody about it, but it started to get to me. I stopped eating, had trouble sleeping, and when I did sleep, the nightmares—of him looming, threatening me with all kinds of awful stuff—they were horrible. My dad started to notice. Thought I was getting sick like my mom. Wanted to take me to the doctor, but I said it was nothing, that I'd be fine. I didn't want him worrying about me, with my mom so bad, right then.

"I tried being more forceful. Told the mayor we couldn't stop by the swamp, and he couldn't kiss me, anymore. He just laughed, and things got worse." She stopped and looked at Wyatt. "Chief Madison, could I have some water?"

"I'll get it." I needed a break, anyway.

Heavenly Days. Just when you think you're in the loop, as far as what goes on in your town, you hear something like this. Apparently, I didn't have a clue. Even the grapevine hadn't caught wind of this.

I grabbed a couple bottles out of the mini-fridge

near the coffee pot and went back to Wyatt's office.

"Thank you, Miz Mercer." She opened a bottle and took a long drink.

"You're welcome, Susie." I handed the other one to Evey. She smiled her thanks, but didn't open it.

"I don't remember the exact date," Susie said, continuing. "But, the last time I babysat for them, he followed his usual route. We stopped. Then he slid across the seat—he'd never done that before—got real close. I couldn't - didn't - want him that close. He started kissing. Then, his hands…." She dropped her eyes, a deep pink blush flooded her face. "He, he was rubbing them all up and down the front of me, at first. And then he was pinching m-my…." She let out a small sound. "Sorry. It still makes me so mad."

Evey caught her hand again. "They have to know, Suz."

She nodded, and took another long drink. "He pinched my breasts," she blurted. "It hurt, and I was mad, but I was scared that he was going to do more than that, and I didn't want him to. Tried so hard to push him off, but he was too heavy, then he was moving down my belly, and I got sick. I mean: I. Got. Sick.

"Threw up all over him. He started yelling and swearing at me, and then yelled some more. Told me what a stupid slut I was, how I'd tempted him. How was he going to explain the mess to his wife?

"I was crying by then, and too sick to care much what he thought. I told him if he'd listened and stopped kissing me before, there wouldn't be any mess to clean up.

"Then his face went mean. Wicked bad mean. I

got even more scared, but he didn't say anything else. Just took me home and drove off.

"Next day, I called Miz Ellie. Told her I couldn't babysit anymore, cuz I'd got a job at Annetta's. Of course, I hadn't, but after I hung up the phone, I ran all the way to the restaurant, and asked Miz Annetta if I could be a waitress for her afternoon shift and on weekends. I guess she could see how desperate I was, cuz she said yes.

"The mayor would come in all the time, after that, especially when I was on shift. He'd just stare, real hard, mad-like, but he wouldn't say a word.

"I never told anyone, not 'til I heard about Randy. Then Evey and I started really talking details." She looked at her friend. "I'm done."

CHAPTER TWENTY-TWO

EVEY STARTED RIGHT in. "Well, I didn't hear about the babysitting thing until two months into my senior year. Kendall had turned one, the month before. The Patterson's were gone on an extended vacation, to visit some of Mrs. Patterson's relatives, and then tour Europe. At least, that's what she told me the first time I sat for them. She seemed really friendly, then.

"Miz Forbes, the school secretary, called me to the office, about the end of the month … October, like I said. She told me she was starting a new senior list, and was I interested in babysitting the mayor's son. It had worked out really well the year before; they'd kept the same girl the whole year. But, it would only actually be half a year. Anyway, since Susie graduated, they needed another senior."

Wyatt interrupted. "She mentioned Susie's name specifically?"

Evey nodded. "Oh, yeah. She said Susie Chapin had done such an excellent job, the mayor wanted to continue the … uh, tradition—if you can believe that—of using a senior girl."

I had to find out. "So, Miz Forbes never knew what Susie had to put up with?" It was hard to believe no one even suspected. "The Patterson's gave Susie a good report, even though she quit so unexpectedly?"

Evey shook her head. "Miz Forbes never mentioned Susie having any trouble. She seemed relieved that the Patterson's were happy."

"I see."

"I don't know if Ellie ever got suspicious of what he was doing." Susie broke in. "She was the one I called the next morning. She actually asked if I was feeling any better. I guess he'd told her I'd gotten sick in the car, but of course, not why. At least, she never mentioned it, and she treated me the same way as always, anytime I saw her after that."

I sat back in my seat. Thoughtful.

"Evey?" Wyatt prompted. "Is there more?"

"Oh-ho, yes. Much, much more."

She opened the water I'd given her, and took a long draw. "It gets messy from here on out. And, it's embarrassing for me. But, you need to know. Suz and I talked about it a lot before we decided to come in."

"We wanted to before now," Susie jumped in to explain. "But it was— We felt so humiliated. I mean, who would believe us? The mayor's a big shot. But when we heard what happened to Miranda, and since she'd been the next babysitter, we couldn't keep quiet any longer." She looked over at her friend. "We feel really guilty about what happened to her, actually."

"Guilty? Why would you feel guilty?" Wyatt's gaze flicked from one girl to the other.

"If we'd said something sooner, she might still be alive."

"Oh no," I blurted. "No. You can't think that way."

They shook their heads. "If we had come forward. Well, if I had told Miz Forbes what he did to me—or tried to do to me—the first time it happened, she never ever would have given him anymore names."

Susie began to cry. "I should have reported him, the first time he kissed me. But I was— He's so important, and I was just a … just a teenager."

Evey grabbed her hand and held on.

"Remorse aside," Wyatt told them quietly. "It's done and over. You can't change what happened, but you can help stop it from happening again. It wasn't your fault."

Evey took a deep breath and nodded. "You're right. You are. But, it doesn't change how we feel about it."

Susie wiped her eyes, and nodded her agreement.

Evey continued. "Okay. Like I said, I started in October. The first time he stopped on Foggy Bottom Road was in February—our first kiss was on Valentine's Day." She shook her head. "Said that was why, because I hadn't had a date, he wanted to make up for it. Shit.

"Later, when I found out what happened to Susie, I figured that her puking on him might have made him think twice about trying it with me, but perverted as he is, he couldn't help himself. It just took him longer to work up the gumption to do it again.

"From that kiss, though, things escalated. My reaction was different from Susie's. I was flattered. He was good-looking, charming, important, experienced. At the time, I wasn't thinking about his being married, just that he was interested. Like, an older man had the hots for me, ya know? Since I didn't protest, he went from kissing, to petting pretty quick." She paused for another drink. And, after a few minutes of silence, I wondered if she was going to end things there.

She shifted in her seat, clearly uncomfortable, and gave a short laugh. "I had this all rehearsed, ya know? It's harder in front of an audience, especially—sorry, Chief Madison—but especially in front of you and Officer Anderson." She cleared her throat. "So, okay. It was April, or maybe May, he, we, got hot and sweaty in the backseat of his car." We watched her face turn bright red, but she didn't stop. "It's nauseating to think about it now, but I was in seventh heaven for a while. Then it started to wear off, sometime around July, I guess. It got sleazy, really sleazy, and it was hard to look Mrs. Patterson in the eye.

"One night, in early August, I think, we were on the way to my house. He stopped the car, and began the routine, like always. But I'd had enough and told him no. Told him I didn't want him to touch me anymore; that it had to stop.

"First he tried the 'ah, come on, baby,' thing. But I was done. Then he got ugly mean, instantly. Grabbed me by the throat and started to squeeze … hard." Her hand caressed her neck as she remembered. "I thought he was killing me. Maybe that was his intent. All I know is, I couldn't get any air, and passed out. When I came to, I was naked in the bushes, out along Bear Creek Swamp. I'd rolled almost all the way down the bank. He probably figured I'd fallen in. If I had gone into that muck, I'd have drowned. No question. He'd tossed my clothes to the side of the road, so maybe…. I don't know.

"Scared the spit outta me, that's for sure. I called Mrs. Patterson the next morning. Told her I had to quit babysitting. Then I called Suz, asked her what I should do. I needed to stay as far away from him as I could. She told me to go to Annetta's, like the next day, and ask for the afternoon shift. She was going to answer the sign in the window at Sporelli's Bakery, so there'd be a spot open at the restaurant.

"I never told a soul—except for Suz—what we'd done. I didn't even tell her I thought he'd tried to kill me." She glanced at the girl. "Sorry, Suz."

"It's okay, Evey. I don't think I could have told anyone, either."

They briefly joined hands again. Female support structure at work.

"Anytime I see him - even to this day - I turn and go the opposite direction, or cross the street, if at all possible, to avoid being anywhere near him.

"When school started, I knew Miz Forbes was gonna get another list of seniors, and called. Asked her what senior girl she'd picked for the primary sitter spot. I didn't tell her what happened. But I should have.

"She said Miranda Richards was the primary. I remembered seeing her on the cheerleading squad, during pep rallies, and at games when she was a sophomore and junior. One day, when I figured practice was over, I went to talk to her. I explained that I'd been the babysitter the year before. She said she already knew that, was kinda snippy about it, too. I told her to be careful about getting rides home from the mayor, that he'd hit on me. She laughed. I couldn't tell if she believed me, or if she thought I was an idiot. I know she had a rep for being loose with the guys, so maybe she was laughing at my warning." She shrugged.

"I'm so ashamed of what I let him do to me, but he was someone important. I should have been able to trust him. Instead, I was trying to get away from him. He shouldn't have put me in that position. I know I shouldn't have let him, but…."

Susie grabbed Evey's hand, again, and squeezed. "We think, whatever happened to Miranda, the mayor had something to do with it. Because of what happened to us, anyway. That's our opinion."

Evey finished off her water. "He's not fit to be mayor of this town, even if he didn't kill her. He's…." She paused, as though deciding whether to finish the sentence. "He's a piece of slime."

"Yeah," Ricky agreed. "He is."

"I'm just, so, shocked." Was about all I could get out.

Ricky looked like he wanted to hurt something, really badly, and I had a pretty good idea who it was he had in mind.

"I'm really sorry you two had to go through all that. Especially alone."

Evey nodded. "He was very charming, very … suave, and sophisticated, and attractive, and he knew it. He used that, and his social status, to take advantage of us. Made us feel like he couldn't live without us."

"Seems we weren't supposed to live without him," Susie added. "Guess that makes us lucky to be alive."

"Evey, you mentioned that the first time you babysat was in October. That was 2006?" Wyatt consulted his notes.

"Yeah. End of October, '06." She thought for a

Jill S. Behe

minute, then nodded. "I graduated in 2007, so, yeah."

"What did you mean by 'she seemed really friendly, then'?"

She looked at Susie. The other girl shook her head. "The mayor and his wife are not at all the loving couple they would have you believe. In private, they bicker, a lot. Sometimes it's more than just bickering. I've heard pounding on the walls, doors slamming, sometimes even glass breaking, during and after a shouting match."

"I saw it, heard it, too," Susie admitted. "Never right in front of me, though. Once, they were upstairs, probably in their room, it got so bad I thought one of them was going to get hurt. When they came down, they acted like it never happened."

"Mrs. Patterson has a very nasty temper. So does the mayor, but I was shocked at how fast she loses it, and over little things."

"Is there anything else you'd like to add?"

"Yeah." Susie raised her hand, then lowered it with an embarrassed smile. "We did something."

"Nothing I'm going to have to arrest you for, is it?" Wyatt wasn't joking.

She shook her head. "No. We, Evey, called the school secretary and told her not to make anymore senior-girl lists. She didn't ask why, but did have a few nasty things to say. The mayor's name was mentioned, in between some words I didn't even think she knew."

"What's going to happen now?" Evey looked at Wyatt.

We all did.

He stood and turned off the tape recorder, then

glanced at the clock. "Now, I have to get ready for an appointment. If the mayor can't see me, Officer Anderson and I will take a ride out there as soon as he gets back." He shook hands with the girls. "Ladies, thank you for coming in, today. I appreciate the courage it took for you to reveal your stories. It's been … enlightening."

"You're welcome, Chief Madison."

A LITTLE WHILE later, Wyatt came out of his office and up to my desk, hat dangling from his left hand. Preoccupied, he stood, shifting from one foot to the other, not saying anything.

I waited.

Five minutes later, still nothing. Almost like I wasn't there. Finally, I couldn't stand the silence. "Was there something you needed?"

He blinked, as though just realizing where he was. "Hmm? I, uh, I'm going over to talk the Pattersons."

"Yes, I know. You made an appointment with them for 2:30."

"I did. Yes. Mrs. Patterson just called my private line. Apparently, the mayor's been called out of town unexpectedly. She assured me, though, that she'd be there. Sounds fishy. I'll have to reschedule with the mayor, as soon as he's available.

"I'm feeling oddly apprehensive about talking to the mayor's wife about her babysitters. She seems upset about the whole Miranda thing, which is understandable. After the way she acted at the funeral…," he made a helpless gesture. "I don't know that I trust her … feelings.

"I'll be conducting an official investigation, and she's the wife of a town official, so I have to address her formally. That's creepy." He ran a hand through his hair. "We've always been on a first name basis. I've been to their house for dinner, for Pete's sake, and bounced their son on my knee."

Sounded like babbling to me. He's usually more in control than that. To say he was uncomfortable was probably an understatement.

And yes, Ridge Patterson suddenly being unavailable was definitely fishy.

I leaned my elbows on the desk. "You don't want to go over there. I get that." It was a statement. I couldn't blame him; I wouldn't want to, either.

He huffed and smacked his leg with his hat. "No. No, I don't want to go over there. I don't want those girls to have gone through what they did because of that man, but they did. I don't want my friend's daughter to be dead, either, but I don't get a say in the matter." He stopped and stared at his boots, for a moment. "Sorry. I'm frustrated, and angry. I didn't mean to take it out on you."

Sometimes it sucks to be the king.

"You have a right to vent, you know. If you can't let loose with your friends, well, who else is there?"

He gave me a look, but I didn't take it personally.

"Thanks, Maggie, I think. Don't know exactly why I don't want to go. It's routine to question anyone who had contact with the victim. I guess it feels weird because it's the mayor, for one; and knowing he's guilty of a crime, that may or may not have led to her death. And then, to talk to the wife as though you don't know that—"

"Do you want me to go along? Or, I'm sure your rookie officer would." I doubted Ricky wanted to, either. Was probably happy that he didn't have to.

He shook his head. "No. But, thanks." He set his hat on his head and adjusted it. "Hopefully, this won't take long. I'll fill you guys in as soon as I can."

On his way out the door, he turned, winked, and gave me a salute. He knows how much I … admire him, in that hat. I had to fan myself.

"We'll be here."

He waved and was gone.

Something had to break soon.

Didn't it?

It was after five by the time he got back … and he looked pissed. On his way past my desk, he glanced over, took off his hat, and went into his office.

The door slammed shut.

Ricky, writing up a report about a fender-bender out on County Road fifteen, looked up at the unfamiliar sound, then over at me.

He mouthed, 'Uh oh.'

Wyatt didn't show anger. Ever. Well, he might in private, but I don't remember ever seeing it.

A few minutes later, the man stepped outside his door. "I apologize. Could you both come in here, please?"

Ricky and I exchanged a quick look and obeyed.

We hadn't even gotten inside the office before Wyatt began to speak. "I'm not mad, not really. I've got all this aggravation building, and don't know how to get rid of it." He started to pace, but stopped after two passes.

"Maggie told us what Annetta shared with her. I have to conclude, from that, and listening to Evey and Susie earlier today, that Mayor Patterson is now our prime suspect. However, that does not prove he's the killer. I don't even know if I can actually charge him with anything. The girls were over sixteen—the age of consent. They would have to initiate the paperwork to press charges. I'm sure they'd have a case. Then again, it would be his word against theirs." He shook his head. "I could talk to the judge over at the Greene County Courthouse.

"As for my questioning of Mrs. Patterson. She did confirm that their marriage was anything but rosy. When Ridge first suggested they use high school seniors, she felt uncomfortable, but went along with his idea. At the beginning, everything went smooth. The girl the school recommended—Susie—was infatuated with the baby, and got along with her and Ridge, or seemed to. When both the first two teens called to tell her they would no longer be able to sit for Kendall, she was disappointed, but not suspicious. To quote: 'I liked them both. I trusted them to care for my son, without reservation.'

"When Miranda was hired, the trouble started. Ellie didn't come right out and accuse the girl of having an affair with Ridge, but she was definitely more reluctant to talk about her." He stopped and looked at us. "I have a confession."

"A confession? You?"

"I think there's something a little bit odd about Mrs. Patterson."

"That's it? That's your confession?"

Ricky whistled, and leaned back in his chair. "Whatever gave you that idea?"

Wyatt shook his head. "I mentioned to Maggie that I wasn't sure I could trust her. I can't quite put my finger on the exact reason why. But now I'm more convinced. Everything she said was just a little bit too practiced, too rehearsed."

"Like what, for example?"

"Take, for instance: She says Ridge changed at about the time Kendall was six months old, and they started leaving him with a sitter—a teenage sitter. To me, that's a leading statement. To me, it says, I suspect my husband is luring girls to our home with Kendall as the draw, and the girls being the lambs to the slaughter, so to speak.

"Next, she says Ridge always insisted on taking the girls home, even though two of them had their own cars. So that means, what? I suspect my husband may be having sex with them? That just smacks of looking the other way, to me."

"Wyatt—"

"Wait. She never accuses him, never confesses her real thoughts to me, either. But, when she starts to tell me about Miranda, the suspicion ... the mistrust, gets more pronounced. According to her, Ridge's excuses start to sound lame. He takes too long—in her opinion—to come home. She says, this time around she confronts him. He laughs at her. Tells her, basically, that her fears are absurd. How could she possibly think he would do anything untoward with a teenage girl?

"Now, I was never an A-student in English, but 'untoward'? You know anybody else who talks like that?" He shook his head, like 'never mind,' and kept on going.

"You realize this is all speculation, right? Just my personal opinion. But, it's based on the way she gave her answers, and the emphasis she used. Not necessarily the words themselves, but the drive, behind them."

He went to his desk and sat, leaning back in his chair. "Okay, back to Ellie's ... story. She confirmed the banquet scenario, and that the school secretary called Miranda to babysit. Ridge had a fit. He didn't want to use Miranda anymore. She was demanding more money. Here again, the emphasis—the innuendo, if I may—is that it's the girl's fault. She wonders whether Miranda is blackmailing her husband. Are they doing things behind her back? At the same time, Ellie says, Miranda's attitude confuses her. The girl seems just as friendly as always. She also said that Miranda drove her own car that last night." He sat forward, arms on the desk.

"Now, Sunday, late morning, early afternoon, Ridge decided he wanted some alone-time. Told her he was going out to the lake, and he'd be gone a while. Mac has verified that, yes, the mayor was at the lake on Sunday, almost all day. Ellie says he didn't come back until after midnight. He was a wreck—muddy, disheveled—and pretty drunk, to boot.

"His story was that he almost hit someone on Foggy Bottom Road, on his way back from the lake. It was dark, and this person just jumped out at him before disappearing across the road, away from Old Bear Creek Swamp. He got out of his car to traipse around the mucky swampy embankment, but didn't see anyone, so he went back to his car. That might have been about the time Wylie-James went into the swamp.

"Okay. Monday morning, Ellie hears about Miranda and freaks out. Why? Because of how Ridge looked and acted the night before, she's convinced he had something to do with it. Why didn't she call and talk to me about her suspicions? She's afraid of her husband ... so she says.

"So, now, I have to decide. Do I believe her story? Some of it, I'm sure, is true. Other parts?" He shook his head. "Not so much. I need to talk to Ridge; to tell me he was at the lake. I know, yes, Mac substantiated that, but I need Ridge to verify or deny, Ellie's speculative accusations. I need him to explain how he got so filthy." He threw up his hands. "But I can't question him. He isn't available." He slapped them back on the desktop. "And that raises another question. Why is he unavailable? Where did he go so suddenly? What emergency came up, so quick, that an emotionally unstable man would drop everything and run to take care of it?

"By the way, when I left, the First Lady of Mossy Creek was sobbing , and not very convincingly. Says she's going to file for divorce, and move back to Jansen City, to live with her folks."

Wow.

Ricky'd puckered up his mouth, thinking.

My scalp was itchy and I could feel a headache beginning to pound behind my eyes. "Okay, I'm gonna ask this, but I want to make it clear that it isn't a slight to your ability as an investigative officer."

"Doesn't sound good, boss."

"Go ahead. Lay it on me. I can take it."

"Funny." If I'd been closer, I'd've smacked him. "I just…. All that questioning was good and informative…."

"But?"

"But, I didn't hear anything about an alibi."

He looked surprised. "Oh, I thought I mentioned that at the beginning."

"If you did, I missed it."

"Me, too."

"Well then, maybe I didn't." he shrugged. "Okay. I did ask her where she was that night. She says she was home, alone, waiting for Ridge to get back, worrying that he'd been gone so long. She indicated that it was quite possible she may have even been giving Kendall his bath."

I nodded. "Pretty thin, but not surprising. Not verifiable, either."

"True."

"A lot of the people I questioned had similar flimsy excuses," Ricky added. "A few had actual solid, couldn't-have-done-it, alibis."

"So, in essence, we haven't eliminated anyone in particular."

Ricky flipped his notebook shut. "Except the ones who couldn't have done it."

"I mean the ones high up on the suspect list."

"Yes. Of the ones in the top five on our list, we don't have enough to eliminate them." Wyatt leaned back in his chair, again, and rubbed his hands over his face. "Look. It's late, and we're getting punchy. We've had a long rough day. Let's call it a night and meet back here tomorrow, around 10, or so."

"Sure, boss," Ricky nodded, getting to his feet. "I'll run by Tate's on my way home, too. Maybe they have some news on that ring, by now."

"Good idea. And, in the morning, don't forget to stop by the Corner Grocer's and talk to Al."

"I won't. Night, Maggie. Wyatt."

My, "Night, Rick," followed him out the door.

I went to my desk.

It was after eight. Not that late, but we'd expended a lot of energy and I, for one, was exhausted. My body was telling me, in no uncertain terms, it was time to go home and sleep. My feet—unused to the dressy pumps I'd worn all day—were making it known, that if I didn't soon set them free, they were going to go on strike. I contemplated taking the shoes off, but I'd only have to put them back on when…. Oh, crud. When Wyatt took me home. I'd forgotten, again, that I didn't have a car. I'd also almost not remembered that we were supposed to have a date tonight.

I glanced toward his office. He was leaned up against the doorframe, watching me. As soon as we made eye contact, he straightened and started forward.

Butterflies began to flutter hysterically in my belly. Yeah, I know, they were bats before, but they'd morphed. These were definitely butterflies—way more ticklish than bats.

Maybe I wasn't so tired, after all.

"Today didn't pan out the way I wanted," he began, getting closer. "I didn't figure on being here this long. Do you still want to go to dinner, or should we wait until next week?"

I frowned. Why do they make us the bad guy? Usually, they tell us, it's because they want to do what we want to do. But that's not always the case. I sat and indulged myself in observing him, not sure how to answer.

Then it came to me. Men let women make the decisions because we're better at it—not always, mind you, but sometimes—more logical, more practical. Men are so.... Men, have one-track minds.

"I would love to have a meal with you, Wyatt, but today was lots busier, and much longer than usual … for both of us. I'm dressed for a funeral, not a date. You're in uniform. How about a compromise?"

"I'm listening."

"It's only a suggestion."

He gave a nod.

"Today was emotionally draining, which carries over into the physical. But, if you were to take me home now, I'd be too agitated to rest. I need a distraction. Something to help me unwind and relax."

He moved closer and wiggled his eyebrows.

I waggled my finger. "Don't go getting any bright ideas, Romeo. Just hear me out. Annetta's is still open. We could go grab something there; then, since you have to take me home, if you want, I could make a pot of coffee and finish baking the rest of those cookies. Um, mainly because, by the time we finish a meal and get to my house, it will be really late.

"A second suggestion; we call and order something to-go, pick it up and take it to my place. Or third, postpone everything until next week, if your offer still stands, we could do something more like we'd planned for tonight."

He stood, just looking at me. Finally, he shifted. "Let's go." He held out a hand and helped me to my feet. "Wait by the door while I turn off the lights and lock up."

I watched him. He'd not chosen any of my ideas, but something was different. His movements had purpose. Made me giddy. The butterflies were madly dancing. This—tonight—would have been my first official date with Wyatt Madison. I wondered how long he was going to make me wait to find out if we were still on.

I stayed by the door as he went through the building turning off lights, copy machines, and the coffee pot, before making his way back to the front. He reached behind me and turned off the light switch, plunging the room into darkness. I moved to turn the doorknob, but he caught my arm.

Before I had any clue of his intent, he said, "I didn't get to do this this morning." His mouth closed over mine.

Just when I focused enough to respond, he shifted. "Let's go get something to eat. I'm starved."

Flustered, befuddled, and a little annoyed, I nodded. I couldn't have formed words if my life depended on it.

"Maggie?" His voice was low and husky.

I bit my lip. "Hmmm?"

"You excite me."

Talk about a rush. Whoo. "I … I do?" Those darned flutters went into overdrive. Hyperventilation was next, I was certain.

He opened the door. "Yeah, you do. Is it all right

if I do something about that?"

"Oh." My brain was mushy goo. "Absolutely."

"Excellent." He grasped my elbow as I descended the steps. Good thing, too, because my knees were so wobbly I would have fallen. "We should walk to Annetta's. It's a beautiful night." We started down the sidewalk at a fast clip.

"Sure. Okay." I frowned at his pace. He had such long legs, and I was in … painful, heels. "Wyatt?" Maybe I could slow him down just a little bit.

"Yeah?"

"You excite me too, big guy."

At his sudden stop, I just missed stepping on him. He turned to face me, way too intense. "Good. I'm really glad to hear that, Magdalena. How many dates do we have to have, before you'll let me sleep with you?"

Then, he smiled. A smile so hot, it scorched.

How serious was he? I'd been dreaming about him for the past year. Melt the walls fantasies. Here was my chance to make those dreams reality. At the same time, I didn't want him to think I was fast and loose.

He must have read my mind. "Maggie, we're both adults. We've both been married. I don't want to take advantage of you, but I've been, well, I've been having some pretty vivid dreams about you, for about a year now."

I raised my eyebrows. Wow. Him, too.

"Hell, I noticed you in high school, but you were with Bernie Mercer. Then again when I came back, almost before I was free to look around. If you want to wait, I'll understand. Just be warned, I'm going to use every opportunity I get to make you hot and bothered, until you can't take it anymore."

I had to smile. Wow. All these revelations. High school? Geez. His promise stepping up the onslaught was telling, too. But, it wouldn't take that long. If this week was any indication of how he'd make my life miserable when he wasn't even trying, I could only imagine how much more frustrated I'd be when he was.

Go for it, Maggie Lou.

"All right, stud, which side of the bed do you prefer?"

CHAPTER TWENTY-FOUR

HE SUCKED IN a breath and bent over at the waist. Shocked, thinking he was having a heart attack or something, I grabbed his arm.

Huh.

"Wyatt? What's wrong?"

He grunted. "Damn, woman. You cut me off at the knees. I'm not sure I can walk straight, right now."

"Oh, come on."

He straightened, not quite all the way, and moved into my personal space until we were almost touching from head to toe.

I could feel his answer before he told me.

"Magdalena," he murmured. "I'm so hot for you right now, it's painful. And, it'll be pretty obvious when we get into a well-lighted area. You shouldn't say things like that without giving a guy some warning."

It was his own fault, though I did have to bite my lip as my body reacted to the way his body was reacting. "You didn't put any sensors on what you said to me. Besides, it's so much more fun this way," I said, a little on the sarcastic side. Then I put my hands flat on his chest and looked up at him, fluttering my eyelashes, over-dramatically. "I guess we'll just have to skip dinner and go right to the dessert."

He closed his eyes and rolled his neck. I thought I

even heard a groan. "Oh man." He recovered pretty quick, and caught my hand. "Let's go, babe. The Jeep's across the street."

Oh, we did go to my place, cuz that's where the cookie dough was. Ha, you thought we were going to have that other kind of dessert, didn't you?

Shame on you.

Y'all, I might liberally speak my mind about most things, but I draw the line at what exactly happens in my bedroom. Although, to be truthful, nothing has in the last ten years or so. Not since my man up and died on me. I just wasn't interested in anyone else until Wyatt crossed my line of sight.

Anyway, you can go right on ahead and fan yourself. Shoot, we were still in the kitchen. Of course, we weren't just baking cookies. I had changed my clothes and was now dressed in my comfy stuff. There were about two trays of cookies to bake, and one was about to come out.

"Maggie, since we kissed last night, I can't stop thinking about you." He held up a hand when I opened my mouth to comment. "I think about you all the time, but this past week, and especially since I got a taste of you last night, it's been non-stop; and not just thoughts. I feel like a hormone-raging teen who just invited you into the back seat of his car."

I rolled my eyes, putting the last drop of dough on the cookie sheet. "My daddy's got a double-barrel shotgun in his closet."

He snorted. "Your daddy couldn't hit the broad side of a barn with a Howitzer."

I wrinkled my nose, picked up the full tray of cookies, and went to the oven as the timer went off. "That's not nice."

"No, but it's true."

I huffed. It was true. "He might not have such a great aim, but he'd give it a good try. Spoil sport." I took out one tray, popped the other in, and set the timer.

"I'm serious, Maggie. I've been itchin' to tell you how I feel. I didn't think … I wasn't sure it was mutual. Then you started flirting back, and I figured I'd give it a shot. I never imagined how … explosive, it would be."

"Me, either. I thought you and Vicki were dating, so I tried to hide how I felt."

"You what? We've never dated, maybe went out once. Whatever gave you that idea?"

I shrugged. Was it all in my imagination? "Different comments she'd make whenever I was in the bakery. But that doesn't matter now. Besides, I decided, when all this mess with Randy happened, that life was too short to waste any opportunities. Something needed to happen, good or bad, and it was up to me. So, I guess I did the same thing you did, gave it a shot. Maybe that's why this feels so big right now, because we both went for it at the same time."

"Maybe. Probably. I'm really glad we found out now."

"Me, too. Especially about Vicki. Less competition."

He shook his head, laughing. "There you go again. I still don't see where you get that I have fans."

"Man," I laughed, slapping my thighs. "For a cop, you sure don't notice much. Every time you walk out the door, people watch you."

"You're nuts."

"Wyatt, I think it's really sexy that you don't pay any attention to all that adoration. You're a very special man. Everyone in town knows it, and appreciates it. I could give you specific instances, particular people, but ya gotta know they're proud to be in your town."

He held up his hand, laughing. "Maggie, stop. You're killing me here. I'm not that special."

I walked over to him and placed my hands on his flat six-pack abs, running them slowly up his torso. I felt his muscles tense. "Wyatt," I said, softly. "You're humble. You don't show off. You respect everyone, until they give you a reason not to. Nobody wants to disappoint Chief of Police Madison. You're a true white-hat wearing good guy. AND dare I say it without freaking you out, I think I'm in love with you."

Wyatt's arms came around me, trapping mine between our bodies, and planted a kiss on me so devastating, my legs turned to rubber. A few minutes later, we both had to come up for air. "Maggie," he groaned. "I really think your view of the world is skewed, but all I care about right now is what you last said."

"Mmm. I was hoping I said it fast enough that you might miss it."

He grasped my arms. "No. Are you? Or, do you

only think so?"

I looked at him. His eyes were bright with hope and fear. I bit my lower lip, and wondered if honesty would end things, or speed them up. "I've been falling for a long time. I love you, Wyatt Madison."

He squashed the air out of my lungs he held me so tight, and buried his face in my hair. "Ah, Maggie. I've waited forever to hear that. I think I fell in love with you the minute I broke out of my fog. I thought at first it was just rebound, you know?" He loosened his hold. "Then, I was afraid to get too close to anyone. I didn't think I could handle the pain again.

"Now, with this murder, I realized that not acting could be just as painful. If anything had happened to you, before I got to tell you how I felt, I'd have…. I'd have…." A deep sigh. "I don't know. I wouldn't have handled it well. Now that I've got you in my arms, I'm not letting go."

I snuggled closer. "I feel the same way. I was so jealous of Vicki. I know you said you weren't interested, but that wasn't until just thc other day. Thanks for telling me, by the way."

"Maggie, I wasn't. I'm not. I never was. She doesn't appeal to me at all. You do. I prefer brunettes … one in particular. And, I like seeing you with your hair down—it's gotten so long in the past year and a half." He kissed me. "But—"

"But?"

"Where do we go from here?"

"What do you mean?"

"Do we date? Do we move in together? I suppose we should have at least one real date before I ask you to marry me."

I blinked. Had I heard him right? Was he really proposing? He had teased about it the other night, with the cookies. Had he meant it then, too? Wow. "Marry?" My voice cracked, and I inched backwards, out of his arms. "You want to marry me?" He loosened his hold, but only because I was insisting. "Yes, Maggie. I want to be with you. I want us legally tied to each other. We're mature enough, and I believe we know each other well enough from working together. Don't you think? You will, won't you? You'll be my wife?"

"I just got used to the idea of going on a date with you. Now you're proposing marriage. I need to sit down. I need a drink. Is there any coffee left?" Holy Cow. I wasn't joking. He'd caught me way far far off guard. This was serious stuff, and he wanted a serious answer, right now. I wanted more than anything to say yes. But was it too soon? My brain needed time to absorb it.

At the counter, I poured a cup, went to the table and sat.

"I'm not laughing, Maggie."

"Neither am I. I'm speechless, honored, elated, unbelievably turned-on, so happy I don't know what to do. All those things, all rolled up into one big emotion. So big I don't know how to express it."

"For a minute there, I thought you were going to turn me down." There was relief in his voice.

"Fat chance, Bub. It came out of your mouth, it's set in concrete."

"So, why haven't you answered my question?"

I held the cup between my suddenly icy fingers. "I will, I promise. I can. I know I can. I want to, so very much. I just, I need to let it sink in."

He came over to my chair and dragged me out of it. "Maggie, I'm in agony. Please."

I didn't know how to answer. I'd waited so long for a positive reaction from him, and now that he'd made one, a huge one, I was backing off. Why? Nerves? Of course, I wanted to be his wife. Why couldn't I say it out loud?

My thoughts abruptly refocused when I felt his hands under the edge of my shirt, and his lips millimeters from mine. I sucked in a breath at the warmness of skin on skin. "Wyatt," I breathed against his mouth. He explored my ribcage, and my belly, and then those talented fingers skimmed across my back, up to my bra band.

He leaned away to look at me, and I saw the question—the please may I—in his eyes. I nodded and kissed him. He made very quick work of those four hooks, and smoothed his way up over my shoulder blades.

I was in trouble; knew it the minute his hands began the trek back and he slid them forward toward my breasts. I moaned at the first stroke along the undersides. His thumbs moved independently around my heavy mounds, until he had both hands full. My nipples pebbled beneath his palms.

I couldn't help it; I groaned and leaned closer. The wave of pure sensation went from there to pool between my legs.

Oh, oh. I had forgotten how fabulous it was to be touched by a man who knew what he was doing. And boy, did he ever.

Buzzz.

He never stopped kissing me, nibbling my lips, dancing with my tongue. Then, his hands were gone. I whimpered at the loss.

"It's only temporary, believe me. Ah, Magdalena, you're so beautiful." His ragged voice filled my ear, as he dragged my shirt, and the trailing bra, over my head. There was a brief moment of chill, before he pulled me close again. "Maggie, is there somewhere we might be more comfortable?"

I was so aroused I almost didn't hear him.

Oh, no, that buzzing sound was the oven timer. Shoot. "Wait. I have to take the cookies out." Self-conscious without my shirt, I glanced around for it.

He ogled my breasts, a lecherous gleam in his eye. "I'd say they were already out."

"Very funny."

He deflected my swipe at the tee shirt flung over a chair and, chuckling, waved me toward the stove. "Don't worry about it, Maggie, I'm enjoying the show. Hurry up, before the real cookies burn. I'd like to get back to what we were doing."

I grabbed the oven mitts. "Easy for you to say, you're not half-naked." I took out the tray and looked over my shoulder at him.

He grinned. "I like looking. You have a great body, Maggie. Nothing whatsoever to be ashamed of.

I know my face was red, felt like it was. "Thanks, but I'm not used to parading around like this. It's a little embarrassing, but I'm glad you like what you see."

"Just so we're even—" He whipped off his shirt.

I almost dropped the tray.

With the cookies on the cooling rack, I turned off

the oven and walked toward him, flinging the oven mitts off, suddenly anxious to run my bare hands over all that gorgeous muscle and sun-kissed skin.

"Come here," he growled. "I think I like touching more than looking." He pulled me against him. "I hope the feeling is mutual."

My whole body was humming. "Believe me; I've got no complaints, so far. My room is straight down the hall to the left."

CHAPTER TWENTY-FIVE
SUNDAY, VERY EARLY MORNING....

I WANDERED INTO the kitchen to make coffee. It was early, before sunrise. I hadn't felt so dreamy, so satisfied, so fulfilled, in a long long time. Spending the night with Wyatt couldn't have been better. Comfy, cozy, content. I went to the window and leaned against the frame. Happy. That's the feeling. So foreign, I almost didn't recognize it.

Okay, so I'd been happy with my life before, but always, in the background, there'd been something missing. Now, all the pieces fit. Bernie and I had been high school sweethearts, and I will love him, the memory of him, 'til the day I die. But this thing with Wyatt? This was different, and better. Maybe because we were older.

Oh hush.

More mature.

I gasped in surprise, then purred when his arms circled my waist and pulled me back against his chest, lips nibbling my neck.

"Good morning, Magdalena." His sleepy sexy voice sent shivers down my back.

My hands closed over his. "Good morning."

He turned me in his arms. "What an amazing night. You're perfect."

"We're perfect together."

"Why'd you get up so early?"

I nestled my head under his bewhiskered jaw. "I woke up. You were asleep … didn't want to disturb you."

"I wouldn't have minded, but I have to say, I haven't slept so well in a long while. You're good for me."

"I'm so glad we didn't keep circling each other."

"Me, too."

"Coffee's done. Do you want breakfast?"

"Not yet. I want you again." He separated from me, just the smallest bit. His fingers stroked my chin, coaxing my mouth up to his.

I was ready, giving back as much as I took. Lightheaded and breathless, we stumbled back to my room.

Two hours later, I was back at the coffeepot, making fresh, with a smile on my face. We had showered together, too. What an experience.

Yes, he's a fabulous lover, even more so than in my fantasies. Sorry I had to close the door in your face, but as my mom used to say, 'What goes on in the bedroom, stays in the bedroom.' Let's just leave it at: I'm definitely gonna keep him.

We needed to get to the office, and Wyatt was anxious to check on Ellie Patterson. Did he think she was going to disintegrate, or disappear?

Maybe.

Shirtless, hair still damp, Wyatt stepped into the kitchen just as I was pouring him a cup. My heart did a flip-flop, and I let out a whistle of admiration. "I'm in awe. Really—"

"Shh." He stood in front of me. His hands caressed my arms, then circled up my back to tangle and twine in my hair. "I get zapped with a million volts, every time we touch. I almost can't believe I'm here. That we're together."

"I know. But, it's so cool that we are," I murmured, not wanting to move as he gently massaged the back of my head with his fingertips.

"I wish this case was done and over with so I could spend all day with you."

"Well, we will be together today, just not as intimately as we'd like."

"True enough." He let go with a sigh. "I'm sure Ellie's parents will make sure she's all right. I just want to touch base with them." He picked up the mug from the counter, dribbled some milk in it, and sat down at the table.

He took a drink and looked at me. "So, when are you going to answer my question?"

I sat next to him. "What question?"

"I asked you to marry me last night."

I blinked, twice. "Oh, that one."

"Yeah, that one. I was serious, you know. The magic in your room aside. What happened here last night, between you and me, baby, we're on a whole nother level. I can't live without you, Maggie. I don't want to."

"Ask me again. Please?"

He stood and pulled me to my feet, holding me in a loose embrace, staring into my eyes. "Magdalena Elizabeth Susannah Maria-Louise Mercer, will you do me the honor of taking my name, and being my forever wife, my life-mate?"

Tears welled; my arms circled his neck as I went up on my toes. "Oh, Wyatt. Do you have any idea what it means to me, that you know my whole entire name? Yes." I kissed his mouth. "Yes, yes, yes, you sexy man."

He let out a harsh breath, all the tension draining from his face. "You said yes."

"I most certainly did."

"YES! The lady said yes!" His arms tightened and he swung me in a circle before snuggling me close against him.

I could hear the frantic trip of his heart as we held each other. Mine was racing, too, full and joyous. This was where I belonged.

"Damn, woman, you had me sweating bullets." He kissed my neck, my hair, my ear.

"Couldn't make it too easy. Now, you know, we're gonna have to invite your fan club to the wedding."

He leaned his forehead against mine, and chuckled. "Will you quit with the fan club already?"

"Wyatt, you do know, don't you?"

His arms tensed as he stared into my eyes. "I'm not sure what you're talking about, now, but if it has to do with this fictitious club—"

I stared back, my fingers touching his lips. "I told you before, it's the whole town," I whispered. "Everyone. I know you think I mean just the females, but it's the whole town, Wyatt. That's your fan club. I'm not jealous; I applaud them. I agree with them. You asked me if I was a fan. Yeah, I am. Your number one fan. And seriously, we have to invite the whole club-the whole town-to our wedding. Well, maybe not all, but as many as will fit in the church."

He leaned his head against mine. "Baby, you

humble me. Yeah, I thought you were just making jokes about how the women react. I can't help it if they take it the wrong way when I tip my hat, hold a door, or wave. My mama taught me manners … a dying art these days. Now you say it's not just women? I didn't realize…. Everybody, huh? Wow." He shrugged, in his unassuming way. "I don't know what to say except; I'm glad they like the job I'm doing."

"Sorry, big guy, but they like you for more than that. Anyway, I just wanted you to understand that it wasn't me being paranoid, or anything." I moved, just a smidge, and kissed his mouth. "Come on. We better get going. The sooner we wrap things up, the sooner we can be alone together, again."

He smiled, eyes twinkling. "What an excellent idea." He let go and started out of the kitchen.

I raced him down the hall.

CHAPTER TWENTY-SIX
SUNDAY, LATE MORNING....

WE GOT TO the office around nine. Ricky wasn't in yet, which was expected. Wyatt had said around ten.

"I'm sure Ricky will have info for us, once he gets here. Just come on back, then."

"Want me to go for donuts?"

"Nah. I think we can do without today. Did you get a chance to go through the rest of the diary? We didn't talk much business last night."

"As well we shouldn't. We were supposed to be on a date."

"Technically—"

"Yes," I interrupted, not wanting to hear the technicality. "I finished reading the diary."

I guess I must've changed the inflection in my voice, or something, because one eyebrow went up.

"Something interesting pop up?"

I snorted—very unladylike—and shook my head. "Wyatt, don't use that phrase in conjunction with that book, please. I'll not be able to keep a straight face."

He tried to hide a smile. "That bad, huh?"

"Worse. Seriously."

"Sorry, Maggie. Any clues we should be aware of?"

"I think so. In fact…. Well, we should wait 'til Ricky gets here."

"Fine by me. Would you mind making coffee?"

"I don't mind, no." Even if he'd said he was going to make it, I would've taken over. One thing Wyatt DOESN'T do well, is make coffee. Not sure why that is, he's so good at everything else.

"Thanks."

"Sure."

Forty-five minutes later, Ricky arrived. "Mornin', Maggie."

"Mornin', Officer Anderson. Wyatt said to come on back when you got here."

He tossed his hat on his desk.

Wyatt looked up as we filed in.

"Mornin', Rick."

"Wyatt." Ricky nodded and sat down. "I woulda been here sooner, but the store didn't open 'til 9:30."

"We're not on a formal schedule today. You're not late."

I tried to see into Wyatt's cup. "You need a refill before we get started?"

"I'm good, thanks." He saluted me with it, and took a sip. "Whatcha got, Rick?"

"First off: I stopped at Tate's last night. Mike said he cleaned the ring with a special acid and the etchings got clear enough to read. It's a high school class ring from 1986. He called the company that manufactured the ring, to see if they still had a record of which school ordered it. Some place up north, New Hampshire, I think he said."

That sounded really familiar. "Hang on." I hurried out to my computer and pulled up Mayor Patterson's personnel file.

Yeah, I can do that.

Aha! Just as I thought. I printed the front page and

went back to the table, handing the sheet to Wyatt.

He glanced at me, then read off the paper. "Ridge Patterson graduated from Manchester Memorial High School in 1986. Well, that solves that mystery. He gave her his class ring, like he was still a student and wanted to go steady?"

"Well, he couldn't give her a wedding ring," I reasoned. "Could be symbolic. As sick as their relationship was, they may have pretended they were, I don't know, promised to each other?"

"Yeah, could be. I can't see her stealing it from him," Ricky said thoughtfully. "Although, babysitting is pretty solitary with lots of time to browse through the house ... or the master bedroom, after the kid's asleep."

"And you would know that, how?"

He glared, then shrugged. "My sister used to make comments about how boring it was, sometimes."

"Ah. That would explain it. There for a minute, thought you might have first-hand knowledge."

"Ha ha ha, very funny. You're such a comedian, Wyatt."

"I thought so. Thanks. What about The Corner Grocer's? Was Al in?"

"Oh, yeah. He confirmed Dodge's sighting, all right. Not that we doubted it. Said the mayor came in late morning on Saturday, and picked up a couple six packs of Yuengling Original Black and Tan."

"Really? He's got good taste in brews, anyway. Didn't know they stocked that over there, though."

"They don't. Al has to special order it, just for the mayor. Only kind he'll drink."

217

"Sounds like Old Man Hornsby. Old coot wouldn't drink anything but Genesee Cream Ale. Rotgut, if you ask me, but he liked it. Had to bring it in from New York, because no one around here carried it. Made a trip north every other month or so and stocked up."

"I remember that old codger." Ricky slouched in his chair, grinning. "He used t' target practice off his front porch. Tore up every 'No Trespassing' sign the Prescott's ever posted, and didn't even have to leave his yard."

"Your uncle used to go out there about once a week, Wyatt, and threaten to confiscate his rabbit gun." I laughed.

We sat pleasantly reminiscing for a few minutes before Wyatt brought us brusquely back to the present.

"Maggie. What else did you learn from that diary?"

I curled my lip at him, but he just gave me that 'come on, come on' motion with his hand. I opened my notebook. "The most interesting was that Miranda thought someone was following her around, getting into her room, and going through her things."

Ricky sat up a little straighter. "Did she say who it was?"

"She didn't report it?" Wyatt sounded irritated.

I shook my head. "No and no. She did mention a couple people she thought might have done it. But it definitely was not Ridge Patterson."

"Really? Then who?"

"Someone slim … small. I'd like to run a scenario by y'all, okay?" I glanced at Wyatt and could almost see the wheels turning behind his eyes.

"Sure. Why not?" He leaned back in his chair.

Ricky crossed his arms. "I'm all ears."

"I'm going to read from three different days. Something about them caught my attention, and they'll explain Miranda's need for a decoy. The first one's from about a month ago. Someone's been in the house. In my room. It's not Dad, he'd feel too guilty about invading my privacy. My stuff's been moved around, not a lot, but I can tell. Somebody was looking for something, probably this book. That means I'll have to hide this, and make another to use as bait to throw them off. Should've done it before now. Might have been Danny, looking for something juicy to write. He got pretty ticked when we stopped having sex.

"This one's a week after. I thought I saw someone sneaking out the back just as I got home, all hunched up in a jeans jacket. The decoy was not where I left it. Coulda been a girl, or a guy … a real slim guy. A guy like Danny. I wouldn't put it past him to do something like that. And, I can't think of anyone else it could be. None of my real friends … I don't think. It's a pretty big stretch, but I almost wonder if the snobbish, supposedly prudish Miss Ellie would stoop so low? She's been acting really strange lately. Not that I blame her. She can't know … can she? I'll have to ask Ridge. It would be way out of her comfort zone to do something like that. And I can't say I even really think it might be her. But…."

I flipped through a couple pages. "Now, this is from the day before her murder. Ridge called and asked to meet me at our rendezvous spot. Then we took my car to the swimming hole. He said it was getting too dangerous for me to babysit for them. He thought Ellie was getting suspicious. I don't think she's starting to wonder, I think she knows. I told Ridge about the baby. He wasn't very happy about it, got really upset, actually, especially when he asked how it happened, cuz he thought I was on the pill. I told him I couldn't wait; I wanted his baby growing inside me. He'd wanted to wait a while, so he could get his divorce. I could have told him Ellie won't give him one, but he wouldn't have believed me. I told him I thought this would force her to realize how serious he is about me. Ridge doesn't think so. I'm sure someone followed us out to the swimming hole, too. I told him that, but he didn't see any other cars, or anyone lurking around. It was really creepy. We left right after I told him, so I think he might have been feeling weird, too. I dropped him off at his car and came home. I wish he wasn't so mad about the baby.

I closed the little pink journal and laid it on the table. Wyatt and Ricky watched.

"Personal opinion only." I held up my hand. "First, I have a hard time imagining Ellie Patterson slinking around through backyards, on the best of days. But, she would have a viable motive, if she knew about the affair.

"Second, the fact that Miranda thought they were followed when they were out at the swimming hole, makes me wonder if it wasn't the Mrs. Mayor.

"Third, should we really consider Danny as a suspect?"

"I don't know. Sounds like a good candidate,"

Ricky said, rifling through his notebook. "He didn't have much of an alibi when I questioned him."

"Really? What was it?"

"Says he was following up on a lead about those mailbox bashings. Went out Foggy Bottom Road and hid in the brush around the Peters's place. He could see the Blanchard's mailbox, too. Unfortunately, no one bothered to come by and he fell asleep."

"That is pretty lame. Why don't you go talk to him again; see if he changes anything he told you."

"Sure. I can do that."

"Well yeah, he's crude, rude, and in your face, but I can't see him breaking and entering, no matter what Miranda thought. As far as killing her? I just don't know. I realize a killer doesn't have a particular look, or even personality, but, Daniel seems too … doofy."

"Doofy?"

"My own description. Dorky, nerdy almost, calculating, conniving, wheedling, whining, etc. You know?"

Wyatt laughed. "I get the picture."

"He comes across as obnoxious most of the time. I suppose, if I were in his age bracket, he might be cute. But, I can't be around him long before I want to smack him. So, no, I don't think he'd have the guts, or the physical fortitude, to hang a girl like Miranda. Although, now that I think about it, that might explain his cold persistence when he saw me at Annetta's."

Wyatt called me back from my musings.

"Hmm? Sorry. Where was I? Oh, yeah. I don't think Danny makes a good suspect." I squinted and looked toward the outer office. I could hear the scritch-scratch of the base radio, and excused myself to answer it.

Shoot.

I didn't want to break up the meeting but, as dispatcher, it was my job to man the radio. "Police dispatch, go ahead." I wondered what kind of emergency was on the other end.

"Mags? Finally. We need Chief Madison."

"Clark?" I shook my head, and tried again. "Danny? Danny Harris? Is that you?"

"Yeah."

"How did you get a hold of a police radio?"

"Long story. Right now, emergency. Need the Chief."

"Who's we?" I let go of the mic to yell for Wyatt.

"Maggie, please." The kid sounded exasperated and desperate.

Wyatt and Ricky came on the run and heard the reporter's next words for themselves.

"Me and a couple friends are out at the swimming hole. The chief needs to get out here. There's blood all over the place, and the only body here is the Mayor's. He's been beat up ... bad."

I blinked, then handed off the receiver, and went to phone the rescue squad as my job training overrode the shock.

I could hear Wyatt talking to Danny. Ricky went to get their gear.

"He's alive?"

"The man's moaning, but he's not conscious I don't think. Doesn't respond to us calling his name, anyway. Hasn't since we got here."

"All right, sit tight. This does not show up in the paper."

"Aw, Geez, Chief. Come on, this is my exclusive."

"And I could arrest you for having an unauthorized police radio."

We all heard him sigh. "Yeah, okay."

"We're on our way. The ambulance might get there ahead of us, but stay put."

"Right."

I was so irritated at Daniel, and so shocked by what he and his friends had found, I almost missed the ringing of the landline. Ricky looked back at me as he and Wyatt ran out the door. I waved him out and answered the phone. "Mossy Creek Police Department."

I heard a muffled sound, and then, "This ... this is Ellie P-Patterson." Her voice was so broken I could barely understand her.

"Mrs. Patterson? What's wrong?"

"I ... I think ... I th-think I k-killed ... m-my husband."

CHAPTER TWENTY-SEVEN

MY JAW DROPPED and I stared at the receiver in my hand, then hastily put it back up to my ear to hear the rest. "He ... he came home right after Chief Madison left, and ... and we started arguing about Randy. I begged him to tell me the truth about what happened to her. He kept saying he didn't do anything. Trying to tell me that she didn't mean anything, the affair. That he loved me, and Kendall, and nothing could come between us. He just made me so mad ... so mad at his lies."

She sobbed.

I took a moment before interrupting her tirade. I used my best, gentlest, most persuasive voice. "Mrs. Patterson, why don't I call Reverend Blanchard and have him bring you over here? We'll get someone to watch Kendall for you, then we can talk face to face? Would that be all right?"

She sniffed and snuffled. "Yes. Yes, that would be all right."

"The chief's out on a call, right now. I'm sure he'll be glad to know you're here, and safe."

That Peacekeepers' Badge—that Wyatt decided I should hang on to—was going to come in handy. God Bless his persistence.

We'd gone around for about a week arguing about whether our 'relationship' would be considered fraternization, or not. He said it wasn't because we were both elected into our positions by the council, and were therefore co-workers, even though he was in charge of the office. I finally gave in.

About fifteen minutes after her phone call, the Reverend ushered a weepy, red-eyed, puffy-faced Ellie Patterson into the police station. Susie Chapin trailed them carrying Kendall. I gave the girl a puzzled look; she just shrugged. Later, I'd think about why that bothered me. Herding the other two toward Wyatt's office, I grabbed the tape recorder, and followed the Reverend and Mrs. Patterson in. Good thing I'd already changed the cassette.

Wyatt's ruminations were still floating in my brain. Was this woman putting on an act? Good possibility. She looked as distraught as she sounded, but—

I pushed the RECORD button and proceeded with the heading for an official report. "This statement is being made by Mrs. Eleanor Patterson, on this twenty-first day of June, 2008, in the presence of the Reverend William Blanchard and Mossy Creek Police Dispatcher Magdalena Mercer. Mrs. Patterson, you stated on the phone that you thought you killed your husband. Is that correct?"

She sniffled into a ragged tissue. "Yes. Yes, I did."

"Did I then suggest you come into the office to make an official statement?"

"Yes, you did. I agreed that that would be a good idea."

"I then suggested that Reverend Blanchard accompany you, and you agreed to that suggestion. Is that correct?"

"Yes, it is. Thank you. His presence is such a

blessing to me, right now. I appreciate you thinking of it."

"Now, because you confessed that you thought you killed your husband, and even though you're only here to make a statement, I need to ask if you would like an attorney present at this time?"

"Oh." She gulped back a sob and blew her nose. "No. No, I don't think I need a lawyer to be here. But thank you for asking."

I gave the Reverend an asking glance. He shrugged and shook his head.

Although I now had official authorization, and was familiar with how to run an interview, I wasn't comfortable in this position. I'd never conducted an interrogation and didn't want to do anything to mess up the investigation. We're a small force in a small town, but there are police protocols and chain-of-evidence rules, and all that other legal stuff. I prayed I was doing it right.

With Wyatt and Ricky both out of the office, there was no other choice. Telling her to come back later wouldn't work—she might just skip town, if my suspicions were correct. And I couldn't stick her in our dinky holding cell and wait for the troops? guys? to return, she wasn't under arrest.

"You're welcome, Mrs. Patterson. Would you state for the record, who you are, and who your husband is?"

"My name is Eleanor Patterson. My husband is Ridge Patterson, Mayor of Mossy Creek."

"Thank you. Now then, what happened to make you think killed your husband?"

Her tears began to flow, again. "Ridge … he said

he wanted to show me what happened, so he took me out to the swimming hole." She waved a limp hand in the general direction. "Out where they found her. He tried to tell me he'd wanted to break it off. Like it was all her fault. I didn't believe him. And then…." She stopped to let out a scream so shrill I had half a mind to plug my fingers in my ears. "Then he tells me she's pregnant. Pregnant! A high school girl, a teenager, pregnant with his baby.

"I couldn't stand the thought of the two of them together. So disgusting, so degrading. And, she made it sound so lovey-dovey. It's sick. Did she really think he was going to leave me? For her? He's so pathetic." Then her voice went low and vicious. "He'd never leave me, even if she did get pregnant on purpose."

Wait. What? Hold on a minute. That sounded— I couldn't stop to analyze that thought; she wasn't finished.

"I screamed at him how much I hated him right then, and he came at me. Started to strangle me. I couldn't breathe. I managed to kick his legs hard enough that he let go. I was so mad, and so scared that he was going to choke me again; I started to hit him with my fists. That didn't do any good. He kept trying to grab at me. I got loose and ran back to the car. The trunk was open, and I saw the tire iron. I grabbed it and turned around. He'd followed me. He was almost on top of me, laughing because he didn't believe I'd really use it. But, I did.

"I hit him with it. Again and again and again." She pounded the table with each word. "I didn't stop. Couldn't stop, not even after he fell and wasn't moving, anymore."

She paused.

The change in her face was like trading masks. Well, maybe it was. Sure seemed calculated to me. Her whole demeanor switched again to drama queen histrionics. The rage was gone, and back was the horrified wife, along with a teeny tiny hint of remorse.

"He … he wasn't … moving. That's, that's when I, when it dawned on me what I'd done. Then I guess I must have panicked. I threw down the tire iron and jumped in the car. There was blood all over me. His blood was all over me. I drove home as fast as I could." She stopped to blow her nose. "When I got there, I went upstairs to check on Kendall. He was still sleeping, so I went to my room and took a shower. I felt so dirty—so very dirty—and ugly, for what I'd done. It's still on me … all that blood; I can't … it won't come off. Then I thought, I should call the police … talk to Chief Madison. He'd just been out at the house, asking questions about … about that girl's death. He'll know what to do, so I can get clean again. That is what I should have done, isn't it?" She looked at me, over at Reverend Blanchard, and then put her head down on the table, sighing, "I'm so very tired."

"Yes, Mrs. Patterson. That's what you should have done." I clicked off the recorder.

The Reverend gaped, pale-faced, shaking his head.

By late afternoon, we were back in Wyatt's office. More subdued, more anxious to solve this case.

Ellie had pleaded self-defense, and Wyatt, though reluctant, released her to her parents. She'd asked me to call them to come get Kendall when she thought Wyatt was going to arrest her. She wept all over the poor man's uniform, thanking him for being so understanding. Her son slept through the excitement.

"I've been speculating about what happened to Ridge Patterson the night Miranda was killed. Tell me if it sounds plausible, okay?"

"Sure, boss." Ricky leaned back and propped his feet on the table.

"All right. According to his wife, he came back from the lake pretty messed up. What if he almost hit Wylie-James? We know they were both in the same area at approximately the same time; at least, they were both on the same road at about the same time. That gives us a window to work with."

That was much too vague for me. "Doesn't tell us who was driving Miranda's car, or how it ended up in the swamp, or who hit Wylie-James in the head."

Wyatt gave me a sour look. "I didn't say it was fool-proof."

"Okay, so which one thunked Wylie-James in the head?"

Wyatt and Ricky shrugged.

"Beats me."

Ricky lowered his feet. "How about: Ridge is driving back from the lake—all lit up, forces a car off the road, then loses control of his own and slides off in a ditch. He gets out to see how bad he's stuck and sees the tail end of Miranda's car going under the muck. He goes over thinking she's inside, but there isn't anybody in it. Then he sees someone climbing up the other side and thinks maybe somebody stole her car for a joy ride and crashed. He goes around and clunks the guy in the head. Then he sees who it is and panics."

"Possibility," Wyatt reasoned, nodding. "And, he's so drunk he can't call it in or he'll get charged with a DUI. But, that's pretty callous of him, to just leave Wylie-James like that."

"Maybe," Ricky speculated, "he intended to call once he got home, but because of his inebriated state, he forgets all about it."

"Okay. But, who was driving Miranda's car?"

My brain itched. Something about Ellie's confession was giving it fits. Leafing randomly through Miranda's diary, I hoped whatever was disturbing my gray cells, would leap from the pages of the girl's mad scribbling and smack me in the face.

Wyatt took a call from the hospital in the middle of our meeting. He then informed us that though the mayor was still alive, there was so much damage to his head, the doctors were not optimistic about his recovery. Brain scans showed very little activity. At this point, if he did survive the next twenty-four hours, he'd be a vegetable.

"So, if Ridge took Ellie out to the swimming hole to confess what he'd done, wouldn't that make him the killer, even though he has an alibi for the time of the murder?"

Wyatt looked up from his note pad. "That's what Ellie told us, Rick, but we don't know if that's true. Sorry. She's pathetic and did a bang-up job of being remorseful, but I don't take anything she says as gospel.

"We have no way to confirm that he actually drank all the beer he bought, but if he was as drunk as he should have been—after twenty-four bottles— there's no way he could have been coordinated enough to hang Miranda. It's a miracle he even made it home in one piece."

"It would be so much easier if he was the killer."

"It would. Yes. Unfortunately, murderers aren't always the obvious choice, no matter how much we wish they were."

I'd not been paying close attention to their conversation, trying as I was to remember what it was Ellie had said during her 'confession' that had snagged my attention. Then, there it was, in bright pink ink. "Of course!"

"What's up?"

"Sorry, I've been wracking my brain for the last few minutes." I rolled my eyes, disgusted that it took so long. "While Ellie was giving her statement, she said something that bothered me. I didn't have time to figure it out, at the time." My fingers tapped the journal. "I just reread a couple of the early entries, from before Miranda hid the real diary.

"Last we talked, remember me telling you how Miranda described everything in super explicit detail, and about how Ridge promised her he would divorce

Ellie, right?"

They nodded.

"Well, Ellie ranted about how ludicrous it was that Ridge would want a divorce to marry Miranda, even if she did get pregnant on purpose. Something in that statement caught my attention at the time, but I couldn't stop to puzzle it out cuz she was still spouting. I finally figured it out."

"Do tell. Pay attention, Rick. I have a feeling, we're about to be enlightened by the stunning sleuthing skills of our very own Miss Maggie."

Ricky grinned. "Hold on, let me get my notepad out."

"You guys are going to pay for that."

"That's okay. I like—"

"Don't even."

Ricky hooted, but otherwise kept quiet.

Wyatt folded his arms and nodded to me. "Go on, Maggie. What did you find?"

"Ellie knew too much."

"About what?"

"If you'd quit interrupting, I'd be able to finish this."

"Sorry. Go on."

"How did she know Ridge wanted to marry Miranda? How did she know the girl was even pregnant, let alone that she'd gotten that way deliberately? We didn't know about the baby until the coroner told us. The only way Eleanor Patterson could have known, was if she had read the diary."

"Ridge could have told her when they were out at the swimming hole. I'm just thinking of possibilities. Doesn't mean that's how it went down."

"You're right, Rick. But, I really doubt he'd admit Miranda was pregnant, especially if—as Ellie told us—he was trying to convince her the affair didn't mean anything, and he wanted her back."

"I see your point."

"There again, we don't know exactly what happened, or who said what. We only have Ellie's version, and we've all agreed her story's too perfect."

"All right, Miss Marple, let's say you're right. What do you conclude?" Wyatt smiled.

I wrinkled my nose. "Ellie Patterson was … is, a very cold, calculating, conniving little snot of a good actress. I don't think she told us the truth. Well, not much, if any at all. I'd say she probably changed most of it around to suit her purpose. So, my conclusion is that she is Miranda's killer."

"Seriously?"

"Oh, the mayor's guilty, but not of Miranda's death. I think Ellie murdered Miranda in a fit of jealous rage, which could give her an out—although I'm fairly certain it was pre-meditated—as was the assault with a deadly weapon, attempted murder, etcetera, etcetera, of her husband."

Wyatt was nodding. "Excellent deduction."

I smiled. "Thank you."

Ricky frowned. "This isn't a game, ya know. Doesn't it make you mad? I'm mad."

"Of course it does." Wyatt answered. "And we're not joking. Do you have a better scenario?"

"No. Yes. No. I don't know. Maybe I'm too sympathetic. I felt bad for Mrs. Patterson. I was sure the mayor did it, but couldn't figure out a way to break his alibi."

I leaned over and patted his hand. "No such thing as too sympathetic, not in my book. You did a great job, especially the way you handled finding the body."

He rolled his neck. "Yeah, well, some of it still doesn't make sense to me."

"What's bugging you, Rick?"

"How did skinny little Ellie Patterson hoist a healthy muscular cheerleader up to a rope swing over the swimming hole?"

"Maggie? Any suggestions?"

"I can't speak to the state of her present physical condition, but according to the background checks we did, she won several trophies while on her high school gymnastic team. In fact, she went to college on a full scholarship. I'm thinking she has, a lot more upper-body strength than we give her credit for. That, and the kick of adrenalin, probably gave her enough muscle to pull Miranda up."

"I agree, but there's more." Wyatt had the case file open in front of him. "She majored in science, so she would know and understand the mechanics of a pulley-fulcrum system."

Ricky folded his arms over his chest. "Which means, she'd know what to buy in order to build a lever system by herself. It's starting to make sense, now. I couldn't picture her.... Well, never mind. But, how do we prove it?"

"Ed's hardware would be the most likely place to buy the items she'd need. Check with Ed or Harlan, see if they remember her coming in."

"You want me to do that now?" Ricky looked at his watch. "They're open."

"Sure." Wyatt made a note. "We need all the physical evidence we can get."

"She's already confessed, more or less, but that may not stand up in court."

"First things first. Ricky, we're about ready to wrap this up. I still want you to go over to the hardware store, and get as much information as you can, just not yet. Based on the verbal evidence— gathered and recorded by our very own receptionist— I agree with Maggie that Ellie Patterson is our murderer." Wyatt slapped the file closed, pushed back his chair, and stood. "I also think that she is so confident of her acting abilities, she is certain she got away with murder. That will make this all the sweeter."

Ricky frowned at me. "Make what sweeter?"

I didn't know what Wyatt had in mind, but grinned.

He smiled at the rookie. "The best way to catch a killer is off guard. I have no doubt it'll be a real big surprise when we show up. Officer Anderson, go get your hat. We're going to arrest the mayor's wife."

CHAPTER TWENTY-EIGHT

JUST AN UPDATE on what's happened the last few weeks.

After our tête-à-tête in the office that Sunday, Wyatt and Ricky took off for Ellie Patterson's house, siren shrilling. About two miles out, they cut it off, not wanting to give her any warning.

Wyatt went up to the door, calm as you please, with Ricky right behind, and asked to speak with Ellie. Her father led them to the dining room, where the family was having supper. Without preamble, Wyatt asked her to please stand, and then read her her rights.

Ricky told me after that first gasp of shock, she broke into tears, just like before. Wyatt cuffed her, and the ranting and raving began. He told her to be quiet, that she could say her piece once she got to the station.

Back in the conference room, Wyatt set up the recorder. This time he asked her if she wanted a lawyer. Subdued and hoarse, by now, she said no, again, and proceeded to confess to killing Miranda, and to beating and almost killing her husband—though she had thought she'd succeeded.

She said Miranda didn't want to cooperate (I wonder why) and accidently hit her head on the desk, trying to get away. Ellie thought the fall killed the little interloper, and that maybe she could twist it to look like suicide.

Who would ever suspect the mayor's wife of complicity?

Just for spite, she'd stripped idiot meddler, and redressed her in the cheerleader suit. She got spooked when Miranda revived. She couldn't let her live, there was too much at stake, and so the strangling commenced. Commenting on how much harder it was than she imagined it would be—and to lug the disgusting girl out and down the stairs—she said using Miranda's car was an ingenious change in plans, and dumped the girl in the trunk.

The swimming hole was expedient and secluded, but public enough that someone would find the slutty teen quickly. Once there though, Miranda came to, again. Ellie was spooked and furious. No way could she let the girl go, not now. Miranda would ruin her life, if she recovered.

Ellie, putting her science knowledge into play, used the big over-hanging branch of the oak tree as a pulley, hauled the rope up, then watched as her nemesis kicked and twisted, and then stopped moving.

How cold do you have to be in order to watch something like that?

I know, right?

She started to drive back to Miranda's house, but decided to ditch the car. Old Bear Creek Swamp was on the right, so she got as close to the edge as she could. That backfired somewhat. Her jacket caught in the door when she jumped out, after putting the car in neutral and rolling it down the bank. She couldn't get free in time, and the momentum pulled her along and into the muck.

Once she staggered out of the swamp and up on the road, some drunk almost ran her over. Back at home, every time she looked at Ridge, she remembered what he'd done with Miranda. The funeral though, was the last straw. With the way her husband was acting, she realized Ridge really did love that promiscuous home wrecker. Ellie wanted him to pay.

It was her idea to go out to the swimming hole, where she told him what she'd done. Apparently, he went a little mad, and tried to strangle her.

I would have too, I think.

Brandishing her conveniently prearranged weapon—the tire iron—Ellie hit him, and hit him, and hit him. When she finally stopped, and the red haze of rage began to clear, she had the presence of mind to realize she might need a good story. Since the cheater was dead and couldn't contradict her, she could claim self-defense, and get away with two murders.

What a sick bitch.

Wyatt formally charged her with the premeditated murder of Miranda Richards, and the aggravated assault, assault with a deadly weapon, and attempted murder of Ridge Patterson, for a start. Wyatt put her in the patrol car and Rick drove her up to the county lockup in Waynesburg for holding.

Ridge, irreparably brain damaged, and with no living will, became a patient at The Sundale Nursing Home down in Morgantown, West Virginia. Ellie wouldn't pull the plug, or allow the doctors to do it, since she was the reason he was there in the first place. It might be a guilty conscience, or maybe she just wants him to continue to suffer—although he's far beyond that ability.

Either way, she refuses to talk about it anymore. She did sign over custody of Kendall to her parents.

Ricky's talk with Harlan Bates, manager of the hardware store, proved to be a gold mine. The man even made us copies of the receipts proving Ellie'd bought the tackle and rope used to kill Miranda. Which, pretty much, left no doubt the woman would be going away for very long time.

The DA's talking life without parole.

Because of his condition, Ridge escaped prosecution by the skin of his chin. Though I'm sure, if he had the wherewithal to choose, would opt for jail time over his present state.

Annetta mentioned she saw a FOR SALE sign on the front lawn of the mayor's house. No doubt, Ellie's going to need the money for her defense.

Mac went to visit. Not a good idea.

He started raging … sobbing, about how Ellie'd taken his only child, and the only grandchild he would ever have. Officers at the jail had to pull him off the bars and escort him from the building. He's now going to grief counseling, and spending a lot of time out at the lake.

Wyatt's keeping an eye on him. He made Mac start carrying a cell phone—turned on and charged at all times. Since their second Binging event, this time with a couple more of their mutual buddies, Mac's been looking better, too; not so gaunt and ragged, anymore.

I'm going over to his place next week, with Annetta and some other ladies from the church. We'll be cleaning out Miranda's room, sans Mac's keepsakes. Everything else goes to the Salvation Army. Once that's done and over with, Mac's putting the house on the market. He wants something smaller, and without the memories.

Men. God Bless 'em.

He'll always have the memories, they're impossible to outrun. Over time, they mellow and the sharpness fades, becoming cherished bits of history— ones we want to keep and wish were clearer.

Wyatt reopened the swimming hole.

The heat and humidity of summer is upon us, and the refreshing cold mountain melt is a welcome relief. Mac and that man of mine put up a small memorial to Miranda, on a particular big oak that shades the pool.

It looks great.

The Town Council's having an emergency meeting in the next few days (supposedly), to elect a new mayor. I told Wyatt to be careful, or someone would nominate him. He doesn't believe me. It wouldn't take but one little whisper in a certain someone's ear, and the job would be his. He doesn't want it, though. He likes being police chief too much.

And, I sure won't be the one doing the whispering. I don't want him to be mayor, either.

Geez.

Can you see me as the First Lady of Mossy Creek?

Hey, I'm sure you didn't mean to spray coffee all in my face.

Wylie-James is home from the hospital. There's still a big bruise on his head, but it's that yucky yellow-green color, that usually means its healing fast. BJ told the man, in no uncertain terms, that he was moving in to keep an eye on his only living grandfather.

Granddad made no protest.

Speaking of BJ, he and Evey Peters have begun dating. They make a really cute couple. BJ got a haircut and shaved his almost beard. He looks downright spiffy.

Working part-time at the restaurant, Evey's recovering. Annetta's talking about giving her full-time. The girl has lost that scared, deer-in-the-headlights look.

That's a good thing.

Susie surprised me the other day. Came by to say hello and thank us again for our help and support. All the bags she brought in made a mess in the office. The aftermath of stress shopping, so she said. Seems Danny Harris asked her out and she's nervous.

Can you believe it? Danny Harris, of all people. Hope his move to date isn't a lame attempt at landing a story about her experiences with the former Mayor of Mossy Creek. (I'd have something to say—or do— to him, then.) I'm secretly hoping she gets wise and dumps him. She deserves better than that snarky little pipsqueak.

I finally got a chance to ask her how she happened to be carrying little Kendall that Sunday afternoon. She said she'd been about to leave the church after choir practice, when my call came through Reverend Blanchard. He saw her in the parking lot, and asked if she'd mind watching the boy while his mother was talking to me. Armed only with the limited details I'd given him, he'd revealed a bit about the situation. She felt sorry for Kendall and agreed.

Ricky, too, took the dating plunge, asking Lancy Farnsworth to dinner—to help him celebrate his twenty-sixth birthday. He told me he'd had his eye on her in high school, but as she was such a popular cheerleader, he didn't think she'd give him the time of day. When he told her that, she'd smacked his arm, and stomped off. He couldn't understand why.

I suggested that she'd probably had her eye on him at the same time, but since he was such a popular football player, she didn't think he'd give her the time of day.

I don't think he got it.

Lancy did agree to the dinner date, though.

I'm not worried. They look good together, and she's got enough sass, spunk, and ditzy, to keep him on his toes.

Officer Anderson and Chief of Police Madison paid a visit to Plain Jane's Beauty Parlor, surprising Forsythia Morgan while her Sunday-go-t'-meetin' hairdo was being arranged. Miss Jane Pratt (who, incidentally, wears those fifties-style cat-glasses on purpose, and ain't too plain, a t'all) had only gotten half the woman's rollers in before our two buff law enforcement officers—with at least five of her grapevine members watching—served her with an arrest warrant.

Ricky slapped on the cuffs and quoted her the Miranda Rights. Wyatt had to hold her up—she liked to have fainted dead away from mortification.

To top it all off, she had to spend the night in jail. Seems her lawyer was unavailable, for at least twenty-four hours.

Only time will tell if it made a dent in her proclivity to spread rumors.

Miss Vera-Mae is healing nicely—that big bulky bandage is gone. We've seen her in town several times in the last few weeks. She stopped in to make sure we had the new number of the phone she had installed last Thursday.

Wyatt is very relieved.

My bestie will be home next weekend. Can't wait! We've got a lot of catching up to do. Yeah she may be mad that I didn't call and bend her ear about it when it was all happening. But, as I said earlier, I couldn't ruin her vacation.

Chief Madison and I have another official date lined up. Actually, we've been seeing each other quite often since our 'first date,' and not just at work. Even without Forsythia, the grapevine is hard at work speculating about what's going on with us.

We're just fine, thank you.

Speaking of…. I gotta cut this short, he's waiting. He wants to go over to Wal-Mart and look at sheets. I don't know if that's bed sheets or baking sheets.

Who cares?

It's been fun. Hope y'all enjoyed your stay. If you ever get bored, come on back and see us again.

You take care now.

Jill is the eldest of four children born to Christian parents in East Central Pennsylvania. It took a while, but the rebel within finally broke free. After shocking family and friends by enlisting in the U.S. Army, then marrying—not much of a shock—birthing three sons, and getting divorced—again, not much of a shock—she's now living in the great State of PA ... at least until the next adventure.

She began writing nonsense stories for her siblings and friends while in grade school, probably from the time she learned cursive. Her writing has improved since then. Thank goodness. With time, maturity, and persistence, Jill continues to hone her craft in a variety of genres.

Taking up the challenge to write outside the box, Jill's story "How Do You Do It, Mr. Sullivan?" was accepted for the anthology Midnight Movie Creature Feature 2. She also co-authored "S.P.Q.R." with Rob M. Miller for the anthology Fifty Shades of Decay. Her newest short, "Whiskers" was accepted for the anthology From Dusk Til Dawn.

Currently, she's working on the third installment of her "Mossy Creek" trilogy (a cozy romantic-suspense), and other projects.

Do visit her at :**www.therebelwriter.wordpress.com**

Also By Jill:

Coming Soon!

Also By DevilDog Press

www.devildogpress.com

Zombie Fallout by Mark Tufo

Burkheart Witch Saga Set By Christine Sutton

The Hollowing By Travis Tufo

Chelsea Avenue By Armand Rosamilia

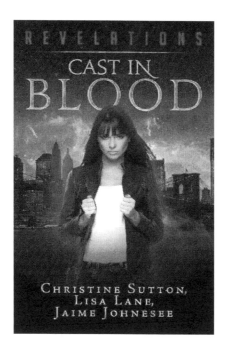

Revelations: Cast In Blood By Christine Sutton,
Lisa Lane, Jaime Johnesee

Thank you for reading Mossy Creek. Gaining exposure as an independent author relies mostly on word-of-mouth; please consider leaving a review wherever you purchased this story.

Made in the USA
Middletown, DE
25 May 2017